BOOK 1

HIGH SIERRA ADVENTURE

S · E · R · I · E · S

THE Legend OF THE Great Grizzly

Jeff Nesbit

D1026401

OLIVER NELSON

THOMAS NELSON PUBLISHERS
Nashville · Atlanta · London · Vancouver

Copyright © 1994 by Jeffrey A. Nesbit

Published in Nashville, Tennessee, by Thomas Nelson, Inc., Publishers, and distributed in Canada by Word Communications, Ltd., Richmond, British Columbia.

Printed in the United States of America.

Library of Congress Cataloging-in-Publication Data

Nesbit, Jeffrey Asher.
The legend of the Great Grizzly / Jeff Nesbit.
p. cm.— (The High Sierra adventure series ; bk. 1)
Summary: When he moves from Washington, D.C., to California's High Sierra country where his new stepfather is a park ranger, twelve-year-old Josh becomes involved in the search for a bear that has mauled several people.
ISBN 0-8407-9254-9 (pbk.)
[1. Sierra Nevada (Calif. and Nev.)—Fiction.
2. Bears—Fiction. 3. Stepfathers—Fiction.
4. Christian life—Fiction.] I. Title. II. Series:
Nesbit, Jeffrey A. High Sierra adventure series ;
bk. 1.
PZ7.N4378Le 1994
[Fic]—dc20
                                    93-39765
                                       CIP
                                        AC

1 2 3 4 5 6 — 99 98 97 96 95 94

Casey,

From the very first moment, I knew.
Always there.
Always willing to listen.
Never too tired to understand.
Forever patient with those in your care.
The world is yours,
Yet you give more than you take.
"Love suffers long and is kind . . .
bears all things,
believes all things,
hopes all things,
endures all things."
Thank you for believing when no one did.
I will always remember.

Books in the High Sierra Adventure Series

The Legend of the Great Grizzly (Book One)
Cougar Chase (Book Two)
Setting the Trap (Book Three)
Mountaintop Rescue (Book Four)

△

CHAPTER 1

△I gripped a small rock ledge firmly and looked down. *How in the world did I get here?* I thought, trying to still the growing panic in my mind.

I could feel my hands becoming slick with sweat. That wouldn't do. Not here, not now, not halfway up the side of a mountain with nothing beneath me but jagged rocks.

I vowed not to look down again. But it was hard not to. I mean, it was a *long* way down, at least a thousand feet.

My mind raced with possibilities. I could keep climbing and hope for a ledge to rest on. That made some sense, because my hands were growing tired from the handholds. I could scoot sideways and hope there was something interesting around a cor-

1

ner. Or I could begin the long descent down. Not all at once, I hoped.

None of the options seemed like a great deal of fun. But climbing higher seemed to make a little more sense. After all, when I'd begun this foolish climb, the mountain hadn't seemed *all* that high. At least, not from the ground.

Now that I was up here, though, it seemed like an eternity to the top. And as I climbed higher, everything began to seem so much steeper.

The first part of the climb had been fun. Easy, carefree, not too hard. I'd climbed five hundred feet without even thinking. Then I'd lost myself in the climb. I'd begun to daydream about what I'd find on the top. I'd thought of other things.

And now here I was, halfway up the side of the mountain with no rescue or haven in sight. As usual, I hadn't planned very well. I only hoped I wouldn't pay a very great price for my foolishness.

I took a deep breath, looked for the next handhold, and began to work my way even higher. Hand by hand, step by step, I worked my way toward the summit.

Except for the wind that periodically whipped around me, there was very little to accompany me on the climb. Every so often, I thought I could hear a bird off in the distance. A few clouds meandered across the sky.

As my hands grew even wearier from the climb, I found myself glancing up with almost every step, hoping to catch some glimpse of the summit.

At last! I spotted a small tree jutting out from the side and what looked like a nest of some sort cradled among its branches. *The top must be just past it*, I thought.

But as I approached the tree, my hope melted away. There was nothing but more rock beyond the tree, as far as the eye could see.

In despair, my head drooped for a moment. I loosened my grip a little. And then, my hand slipped free! Frantically, I tried to grab hold again, but one of my feet slipped from its perch as well.

In the blink of an eye, my other foot slipped off, ripping my remaining hand from the side of the mountain. I began to fall. My mind started to fade to black from the terror that gripped me.

Yet even as I was beginning to black out, I heard the eerie *"Scree!!!"* in a corner of my mind. Hard, strong talons dug through my shirt and tore into my flesh.

I jerked my head around and looked into the blood-red eyes of an eagle. *"Scree!!!"* it screamed a second time as it began to pump its wings hard, slowing the fall . . .

. . . and I bolted upright in my bed. My pajamas were soaked. My heart was pounding like mad. My eyes were now wide open in terror.

Within moments, however, my eyes adjusted to the darkness in my bedroom. I could make out my basketball hoop over my door, and the Super Nintendo in the corner. It was my own room. I wasn't falling to my death from the side of a mountain after all.

I sank back to my pillow and let out a ragged sigh. "Just a dream," I murmured. That eagle! It had seemed so real.

3

There *had* been a time, so very long ago, when I'd climbed the side of a mountain. My dad had been alive then. And I had wandered off on my own, during one of our hikes through the mountains.

But my dad had found me stranded on a ledge just several hundred feet or so up the side of an embankment. He'd scrambled up the slope and carried me down.

Dad had never told Mom about how I'd run off and tried to climb up some rocks on my own. It had been our secret, one that had taught me a hard lesson about obeying your parents when they tell you not to do foolish, dangerous things.

I closed my eyes and thought about sleep. But the image of that eagle kept drifting before me. It had seemed so real, so near. For some reason, I felt certain I would see it again.

△

CHAPTER 2

△The dream and the eagle were a distant memory when I woke up the next day. It was Friday, but school was out for teachers' conferences. It was the day of our big bike race.

We'd spent three weeks mapping out the route—down the long cul-de-sac where I lived, onto the walking path through the woods, across the stream, around the church parking lot, up the tallest hill in the neighborhood, and then down a steep hill to the finish line at our school.

I'd already practiced it three times. I was pretty sure I had all the shortcuts figured. There was no way I was going to lose, I reasoned. No way at all.

At the start, I let my friends get out in front. They all practically mauled each other trying to get to the end of the cul-de-sac first. I waited and let them get out of breath racing to the bottom, then I passed them once we hit the woods.

Two kids crashed trying to get across the stream, and my only other competition skidded out in the church parking lot. I was home free as I got to the big hill.

As I began to climb, though, the memory of my dream the night before suddenly lurched into my mind. The puny hill I was now beginning to climb seemed so tame compared to the mountain I'd been climbing in my dream.

"*Aagghh!*" I yelled. I stood up on my bike and pedaled once, hard, to get a good start up the hill. I pushed the dream from my mind and tried to pay attention to the task at hand.

Halfway up the hill, I stalled just a little. I pedaled harder. I glanced over my shoulder only once to see if anyone was gaining. The front wheel of my BMX hit a pebble, skidded, and then righted itself. I gripped the handlebars harder.

A car roared by. Its horn blared, but I just ignored it. This was my road, too. I had every right to be on it, didn't I?

As I neared the top of the hill, I slowed just enough to look around. I always liked the top of this hill. I could see in almost every direction from this spot.

My head was spinning a little from the rush of the race. *This has to be the top of the world,* I thought as I pedaled slower and caught my breath. There was a shout from behind me. I looked over my shoulder again. Two kids were pedaling furiously to reach the crest of the hill.

I stood up on my bike and gave one furious kick to start down the other side of the hill. I moved my feet as fast as I dared, racing down the other side.

The trees and houses became a blur. I leaned forward and flattened out over the bike to cut the wind drag. There was no way they were going to beat me to the bottom. Not today.

Somewhere, in some corner of my mind, I knew I was going too fast. I was wearing my helmet, but if I wiped out at this speed . . .

I banished the thought from my mind. I wasn't going to wipe out. I almost never did. There was no reason I should now.

The shouts behind me faded. All I heard now was the roar of the wind in my ears. My eyes began to tear up, but I didn't dare risk trying to wipe my eyes. It was too dangerous.

I was just fifty yards from the finish line when the rabbit bolted out onto the road, directly in front of me. The rabbit stopped in the middle of the road, frozen in its tracks. Its tail twitched once. I reacted in a split second.

"Move!" I yelled at the top of my lungs, throwing all my weight onto the brake. The rear end of my bike skidded hard. The tire began to swerve madly to the right, toward the gravel on the side of the road.

The rabbit remained frozen for an instant longer, but then scurried off to the safety of the trees on the other side of the road just in the nick of time. The front tire on the bike missed it by about a foot or so.

7

I had no time to see this, however. I was cranking my handlebars hard to the right to keep the bike up as the back tire continued to fishtail out to the right. I knew that I'd wipe out if I couldn't pull it back.

But I never had a chance. The tires hit the gravel and it was all over. The tires skidded hard, and the bike began to roll. I had just enough time to bail out over the top.

I flew through the air and landed on my back with a mind-numbing *whomp* on the grassy slope in someone's front yard. I heard my bike crashing end over end on the gravel behind me.

My mind was reeling. My whole body hurt from the fall, but I was pretty sure nothing was broken. I took a deep, ragged breath and opened my eyes. My heart was still pounding.

I sat up and looked over at the road. My friends, seeing that I wasn't hurt too badly, didn't even slow down. They raced by, their eyes on the prize in front of them.

I just shook my head. I looked back up the road, but the rabbit was long gone. I raised a fist in the direction where it had vanished into the trees.

"Stupid rabbit," I growled. "You're lucky I stopped. You'd be dead now."

I got to my feet slowly and ambled over to my bike. I looked it over. No major damage. The front fork was bent a little, but I could straighten that out with no problem once I was back home.

I climbed back on and pedaled slowly toward the bottom of the hill, where my friends were waiting for me.

I reached down and jingled my pocket just to

make sure I'd brought some money. Because I'd lost the race, I'd have to buy the winner a Slurpee. That was the deal, like always.

But I could roll it over onto the basketball court. Maybe I could challenge the winner to a double-or-nothing match? *Got to,* I thought. *No way is that dumb rabbit going to cost me a Slurpee.*

"Nice move, Landis," one of my friends called out as I came closer. "Were you showin' off?"

"Didn't you see that rabbit?" I answered, gritting my teeth.

"What rabbit?" one of my friends teased.

"You didn't see me skid trying to miss it?"

"Nah," one of them laughed. "We just saw ya plow your nose into the grass."

I didn't say anything. I coasted past them, jumped the curb, and sailed through an opening in the fence that surrounded our elementary school. I hopped off my bike while it was still moving and let it coast until it fell to the grass on its own.

I ran over to the corner of the school and grabbed the mini-basketball we always stashed behind the bushes. I trotted out onto the basketball court with the eight-foot goals, planted myself there, and waited for my friends to join me.

"Double or nothin'," I yelled defiantly as they drew nearer.

"No way," one of my friends said. "I'm thirsty. I want my Slurpee now."

"Double or nothin'," I persisted stubbornly. I wasn't moving from this court until they agreed.

My friends looked at each other. They knew I wasn't about to leave until I'd gotten my way. The friend who'd won the race sighed and shucked his jacket. He stepped out onto the court.

I grinned from ear to ear and tossed the little basketball to my friend. "Warm up?"

"Nah, let's just play," my friend growled, dribbling once and then making a break for the hoop at one end of the court.

But I'd learned my lesson from the rabbit and I was ready for the unexpected this time. I stepped into my friend's path quickly, blocking him. My friend tried to change directions, but lost the dribble. The ball careened off to the side, out of the court.

"My ball," I crowed as he went to get the ball back. I was certain now. There was absolutely no way I was going to lose this match. The stakes were too high. I only had enough change in my pocket for one Slurpee. I was in big-time trouble if I lost now.

CHAPTER 3

△It was just starting to get dark when I managed to drag myself home. Instinctively, I braced for my mom's yell. I'd missed dinner by a mile. I was sure to get it.

But my dinner was covered with plastic wrap and waiting outside the microwave. Mom wasn't in the kitchen. So I popped the microwave door open, stuffed the plate in, shut the door, and punched in the numbers.

While I waited, I opened the refrigerator door and looked for something to drink. I knew Mom would ask me to pour a glass of milk. But she wasn't around, so I pulled a soda from the back and carried it over to the table.

The house was quiet, which meant that my mom was either upstairs in her bedroom, down in the basement, or out somewhere doing something. Was

I forgetting that there was something going on tonight? Where *was* she, anyway?

There was a month or so of school left until summer break. It was warm enough in the Washington, D.C., suburbs to go without a coat. Mom still made me wear a hat, but I always stuffed it in my pocket as soon as I was out the door.

The microwave beeped. I reached in and grabbed the plate without thinking. "Yikes!" I yelled and pulled my hand back quickly before the hot plate could burn my fingers too badly. I reached in the nearest drawer and pulled out a hotpad.

"You home, Josh?" a voice called from upstairs.

"No, it's Freddy Krueger."

"Who's he?" Mom yelled down the stairs.

"Brother," I muttered. "She doesn't know *anything*."

"I heard that," my mom called down.

I listened to the stairs creak as Mom walked down them. I carried my plate over to the table and sat down quickly. Maybe if I was eating when she walked in, she wouldn't yell at me for being late.

As I put the first bite in my mouth, I was startled to hear a sharp *click-click-click* as Mom walked through the foyer and into the kitchen. I looked up and stared at her.

My mom was pretty normal, as mothers go, I guess. She was only a foot taller than me. She wore her brown hair short, usually wore sweatshirts and jeans around the house, and my friends all thought she was cool because she talked to them like they were grown up.

But tonight was obviously different. She was

wearing a nice dress. She had high heels on. She *never* wore high heels, especially not around the house.

"What's goin' on?" I asked, confused.

Mom frowned. "Don't tell me you forgot about tonight already?"

"What's goin' on tonight?"

"I told you earlier in the week. Mark's taking me to the symphony tonight. Remember?"

I grimaced. Yep, I'd forgotten. Or pushed it out of my mind. Mom sure was seeing a lot of this guy, a whole lot more than she'd ever seen anyone since Dad had died three years ago.

"Oh, yeah, that," I mumbled. "Are you gonna be out most of the night?"

"Yes, and I think Mark's planning to take me out somewhere afterward."

I glared at Mom. What was going on here, anyway? "What's the special occasion?"

Mom didn't answer right away. "We'll talk later, honey. I promise. There are some changes we'll need to talk about. But Mark will be here any second now. This just isn't a good time."

"I don't care!" I said angrily. "You're just gonna leave me here all alone, where some killer on the loose could come in and wipe me out?"

Mom laughed. "I think you'll be fine, Joshua. Really. Lock the doors. Say hi to Freddy Krueger for me."

"You don't even know who Freddy Krueger *is*."

"Sure I do. He's that guy with the hockey mask, right?"

But I wasn't about to be diverted so easily. "So what's the deal with Mark, anyway?"

"The deal?"

"Yeah, you know. Are you, like, real serious about this guy or what?"

Mom smiled warmly. "Yes, Joshy, I'm real serious about him."

"Don't call me that!" I said sharply.

"What? Joshy?"

"Yeah, that. It's a baby name. I'm not a baby anymore. I'm twelve, for cryin' out loud."

Mom's face softened a little. "You're right. You're not a baby anymore. I forget sometimes. I'm sorry."

"Yeah, well, anyway, what's the deal?" I asked gruffly.

"With Mark?"

"No, Ryne Sandberg," I said sarcastically.

"Ryne Sandberg. Who's he?"

I sighed. "You're kidding, right? Didn't you watch the World Series last year? He's only like the greatest second baseman of all time."

"Oh, him. I guess I forgot."

I just shook my head. It was weird sometimes how my mom didn't seem to know things, like who Freddy Krueger or Ryne Sandberg was. Everybody in the whole world knew who they were.

The doorbell rang. I jerked in my chair, like someone had just fired a gun.

"That must be Mark," Mom said.

"Hmmm," I grunted, and turned back to my plate. I pushed the food around while Mom walked to the front door.

I tried to shut it out, but still I could hear the two

of them kissing at the front door. *Gross*, I thought. *I wish she wouldn't do that around me.*

I didn't look up right away as they came back into the kitchen. I just continued to push my food around on the plate, making little piles.

"Hey, Josh!" Mark said, his voice unusually loud. "How's life?"

"OK," I mumbled.

"Break any world records today?"

No, but I almost broke some stupid rabbit's neck, I thought. "Nah, same old," I said, looking up.

Mark was all dressed up, just like Mom. Mark towered over her, and again I felt just a little intimidated by him, like I always did. What in the world was going on here, anyway? What was the big deal?

Mom walked over to me, walking on her tiptoes so her heels wouldn't scuff the kitchen tile, and gave me a quick kiss on the forehead. "It's Friday, honey, so you can stay up late. You don't need to wait up for us."

"And if some lunatic escaped mass-killer convict or something comes around?" I growled.

"Call Nine-one-one," Mom said sweetly, with a smile.

"Yeah, right, like that'll help."

Mom glanced at her watch, and then over at Mark. Mark nodded, as if he could read her mind. "We have to go, Josh," she said. "You'll be all right?"

I rolled my eyes. "Oh, I'll be all right. Don't get in a wreck or anything trying to get there on time."

"Don't worry," Mark said reassuringly. "My Land Rover's like a tank."

15

"We'll talk later? OK?" Mom asked, her eyebrows raised.

"Go," I commanded. "You'll be late."

As they walked past the table to the garage, Mark reached out and gave me an affectionate squeeze on the shoulder. I tried my best not to shudder at the touch.

It wasn't that I didn't like Mark. That wasn't it. I actually liked Mark a lot. He was a cool guy. He liked all sorts of neat, outdoors junk. It just sort of bothered me that he was around my mom so much, that's all.

"See ya," Mom called out. Mark waved. I didn't wave back.

It wasn't until several minutes had passed that it finally dawned on me that I had the entire house to myself for the rest of the night.

Which meant that I could eat chocolate until I was blue in the face, crank the stereo up to the max, and watch music videos until all hours. Maybe this wasn't so bad after all.

Still, I had this feeling that something was going on with Mark and my mom. I'd have to find out. I would definitely have to get to the bottom of this.

CHAPTER 4

△ Even though summer break was still a month or so away, I was already starting to plan for it. I was *definitely* going to play both soccer and Little League, even if I couldn't con Mom into taking me to all of the practices.

My mom complained that it was too hard getting away from work to take me to everything I wanted to do, but she always seemed to find a way, somehow.

I *knew* it was awfully hard trying to work and pay the bills and drag me around to four or five practices a week *and* games on the weekend.

But she just always seemed to be there when I needed her. And when she couldn't be there, she'd arrange for a friend to carpool or something. So I just took it for granted. That was what moms were for, wasn't it? To be there? Especially when your dad wasn't.

My mom and Mark had been out until maybe two or three in the morning the night before. I'd tried to wait up for them, but I'd fallen asleep on the couch watching music videos that had all started to sound the same.

Now, as I lay in bed staring up at the ceiling, listening to the birds outside my window, there was something I just couldn't seem to remember. What was it Mom had said? Something about how we had to talk today?

I glanced over at the clock on my dresser. It was almost ten o'clock. I'd really slept in, like I always did on Saturday when I didn't have anything like a soccer match to go to.

I heard the faint tinkling of dishes in the kitchen, so I knew Mom was up already. I groaned. The thought of actually getting out of bed pained me.

And then I remembered. A cold chill suddenly gripped me. Mom had said we needed to talk about changes. And somehow I just *knew* what kind of changes she had to be talking about.

"No!" I yelled to no one, pushing the covers back violently. I rolled out of bed onto the floor, pushed up off it, grabbed a pair of socks near the bed, and hurried downstairs.

I slowed, though, when I got to the kitchen. There was a brightly colored cloth on the table. There were covered dishes in the middle of it, and blueberry muffins in a basket. There were two plates from the special china set out. There were two full glasses of orange juice. I could smell scrambled eggs.

18

There was also something else on the table. Two things, actually. A small, velvet-covered box and a road atlas. I knew the two were linked, somehow. I *knew* it.

"I wondered if you were ever going to get up," Mom called from the stove without turning around.

I decided not to wait. "What's all of this for, Mom?" I demanded angrily. "Mark coming over or something?"

She still didn't turn around. "No, it's just for us. For the two of us."

"Yeah, well, *why?* You never do this kind of thing."

Mom reached over and flipped the heat off, grabbed the handle of the skillet she was tending, and turned to carry it from the stove to the table. I'd been right. It was scrambled eggs with cheddar cheese, one of my favorites.

Mom paused just long enough to give me a quick kiss on the cheek. "Can't I do something special for my only child every once in a while?" she whispered. "All right?"

"But, Mom," I pleaded. "I *know* something's goin' on here, so I—"

"Let's sit at the table and eat first," she interrupted. "Please?"

I stared hard. But I took my seat at the table without another word. It was obvious she wanted to do this her own way.

"Would you like to say grace?" she asked me. I shook my head, so Mom continued. I closed my eyes and bowed my head. I always liked it when Mom said grace. I liked listening to the easy way she talked to God.

"Lord Jesus," Mom said softly, "we thank You so much for this chance to be together as a family, to talk this morning. May You guide us in our steps and our conversation today. We ask for Your blessing on us this day. Amen."

"Amen," I answered and looked up. Mom had a mile-wide smile on her face. I tried not to let it get to me. But I couldn't. I just couldn't. I started to smile, too.

"So, let's eat," she said. She pushed the basket of muffins over at me and pointed at the eggs.

I ignored all that for the time being, though. I looked over at the little box and the atlas. It was time to get to the bottom of all this. "So what's that all about?" I asked, inclining my head toward the two items.

"Those?" Mom asked innocently.

"Yeah, those," I growled. "What's all this about?"

Mom paused, took a deep breath, and then reached across the table to pick up the atlas. She began to thumb through the pages in the front.

"Josh," she said slowly, "what's the best vacation you've had? Which one was the most fun?"

"I dunno," I mumbled. "Disney World was pretty cool last summer, I guess."

Mom nodded. She'd managed to save up enough for a three-day pass to Disney World last summer. We'd driven down and stayed at a friend's house near Orlando. It had been fun, just the two of us, wandering around the huge amusement park.

20

"Do you remember the last vacation with your dad?" she asked. "Do you remember that?"

I gritted my teeth. I remembered, but it seemed like such a long time ago. Everything with Dad seemed like such a long time ago.

I'd just turned nine that summer. We'd taken a camping trip somewhere for two weeks, the three of us.

Where had we gone? To some big river out west somewhere? Near some mountains? Dad had taught me how to fish, how to fly cast, back and forth, back and forth.

I hadn't caught much, at least not with the fly caster. Dad had taken me to a deeper part of the river, to a pool of some kind, where he'd been able to just plunk a regular old hook, worm, and bobber in. I'd caught a few there.

And we'd gone hiking in the foothills of the mountains, just Dad and me. Mom had stayed behind, at camp. We hiked out and back for an entire day once. We'd seen all kinds of deer that day. It had been great.

My eyes started to get misty. It had been a long, long time since I'd thought about Dad like this. But I could see that vacation in the mountains somewhere more clearly now. Like it was just yesterday. There was Dad, standing in the river with his hip-waders on . . .

"So you remember the trip?" Mom asked, jolting me back to the present.

"Yeah, I remember it," I muttered. "It was fun, out west somewhere, right?"

"Yes, it was." Mom nodded. "We went hiking along the Colorado River for two weeks."

"And there were mountains, too?"

"Yes, there were mountains. Our camp was at the foot of some of the ranges. Your dad liked places like that, outdoors, near rivers and mountains."

I clenched my fists tightly. "Mark likes all that kind of junk, too, doesn't he? He likes all that nature stuff?"

"Yes, Josh, he does," Mom said easily. "You know he does. That's why he's in the National Park Service."

"Is that what all this is about?" I asked, trying not to panic. My throat was getting tight, though. "Is it?"

Mom looked down at the atlas. She'd found the page she was looking for. She slid the atlas over to me. "Josh, take a look at the map. It's the southern part of California. Look east of Fresno, at the mountain ranges and the forest there. It's where the giant sequoias are, where they have some huge rivers and the High Sierra mountain ranges. Wouldn't that be a neat place to live?"

I glanced at the page, but I didn't see it. I didn't want to hear this. Not now. Not ever. I pushed the atlas away. It fell off the table and smacked against the floor. "No! It wouldn't. I like it here in the D.C. area. This is a great place to live. I like it *here*."

"Josh, there's so much more to do in a place like that, so many wonderful things to do—"

"I don't care, Mom," I said, on the edge of tears now. "I like it here, with my friends."

Mom took a deep breath. "You go to junior high

next year. You'll make new friends there. If we were going to move, now would be a good time, wouldn't it?"

"Are we gonna move, Mom? Are we? Is that what this is all about?"

Mom reached over and picked up the little velvet box. She opened it gingerly. There was a diamond ring inside. One of the rays of the sun glanced through it, causing the ring to sparkle. "Mark has asked me to marry him, Josh," she said softly.

"And you said yes, right?" I said, really fighting back the tears now.

"I wanted to talk to you first. I wanted to see what you thought."

One tear trickled out the side of my eye. Then a second came, and a third. I let the tears drip onto my plate. "You really love him, don't you?"

"Yes, I do. Very much. And I think you will, too. If you give it a chance."

"But what about Dad?"

"He would have wanted this. Mark is a good man."

I still fought the tears. "But why do we have to move?"

Mom sighed. "Because the National Park Service wants to send him out to one of the national parks. The High Sierra National Park, in California."

"And we have to go, too, right?"

Mom smiled. "If we're going to be a family, yes. I'm pretty sure I can find another job out there, if I have to."

Time came to a crashing halt. It was almost as if I could see Dad sitting there at the kitchen table with us, like always. Like nothing had happened. But everything had happened. My whole life had been turned upside down and I didn't think it would ever come out right again. Not ever.

I thought about Mark. *There's no way I'm going to forget about Dad!*, I thought bitterly. *You can't make me.*

I just wanted to scream: No! I don't want to do this. I love Dad. I miss him. I wish he was here, right now. I don't want to go hiking in the mountains with Mark, even if he is OK.

I don't want to move. I don't want to. I just want to stay here, where I understand things, where I've figured things out.

Mom said God helped you when things got really tough. Like when Dad died. Mom didn't cry too much, mostly because she said she knew God would take care of him. So was God going to help me understand all of this?

I *wanted* Mom to be happy. I really did. And if it meant agreeing to Mark, well, I knew that eventually I'd have to. It was the right thing to do. I would do my best to honor and obey Mom. I would, even if it killed me. But I didn't have to like it.

"What's the name of the place again?" I asked.

"The High Sierra National Park. Mark says you'll like it."

"And when do we move?"

"As soon as school's out."

I grabbed a muffin, took a big bite, and began to chew slowly. It helped keep me from crying. I looked at the ring. It really was pretty. I knew Mom would be happy. Mark wasn't Dad, but then, I figured there was nobody ever who was going to be like him.

"All right, I guess," I said glumly. "It's OK with me."

Mom reached across the table and gave my hand an affectionate squeeze. Usually I shied away from mushy junk like that. But I didn't today. Today, it was all right.

△

CHAPTER 5

△The last few weeks of school flew by. It was all I could do to pay attention. I found myself just staring off into space all the time, daydreaming about all sorts of weird stuff.

I knew I was supposed to be happy about this. I wanted Mom to be happy. I really did.

But it had been just the two of us for three years. Just Mom and me. And now there would be this third person, who was making us move clear across the country for no good reason.

Actually, I knew this wasn't true. I knew Mark wouldn't make us move if we didn't want to. I was sure of that. Mark was like that. He always asked you what you wanted.

I'd thought about maybe telling Mom that I didn't want to move. But I never said anything. I knew it wouldn't do any good. In the end, we were going to move. There wasn't much I could do about it.

There was this book at school, about different places in the country. The librarian had found it for me during one of my library breaks.

It had a section about the High Sierras and the sequoias. I must have read it and re-read it ten times before I finally gave it back. It did look like a pretty cool place. It sure was different from Washington.

But I was going to miss all of my friends. I'd been planning my summer for so long, and now it was all going right out the window.

My soccer team was in great shape. It had been together for four years now, and we had *almost* won the championship the year before. This year, there was no way we were going to be denied. I was sure of it. But I wasn't going to be a part of it.

We'd begun work on a monster treehouse the summer before, and a couple of my friends had figured out how to actually build a walkway to one of the other nearby trees, like the "lost boys" in *Peter Pan*. But they'd have to build it without me now.

And Mom had promised that we could go to Disney World for an entire week sometime during the summer. I was going to spend as much time as I wanted at Space Mountain, and I was going to go down as many rides as I wanted. But would we come back clear across the country for that now?

The wedding was real small. There was just Mom and Mark, me, my grandparents from North Carolina, and Mark's parents, who flew down from somewhere in Minnesota.

There was a little party afterward, where all the

grownups sat around the kitchen table and talked about the new director of the National Park Service and the cost of new houses in California. I left after a little while and fooled around with my new Super Nintendo game. I was sure no one even noticed me leave.

I didn't hear Mom come into my room, because my game was in the corner of the room and my back was to the door. I was furiously parrying blows from my opponent in the martial arts game. I won, knocking out my opponent, and thrust a fist high in the air.

"You're pretty good at that," Mom said softly.

I jumped a little. "Oh, yeah, I guess. I've been practicin' for a while."

Mom smiled. "I can see that."

I glanced at the door to see if the rest of the party was coming into my room, too, to gawk at my Super Nintendo game. That would be great. But there was no one else there. "How come you're not downstairs at your party?"

"Because I'm up here talking to you."

"Yeah, real funny. You know what I meant."

"I wasn't being funny. I wanted to see how you were doing, how you felt about all this."

I looked back at the game, pretending to study the new characters that had sprung up on the screen. But I couldn't really see their faces very well. "I'm OK," I managed finally.

Mom sighed. "I *know* this is hard, Josh. Really, I do. I know you had your heart set on winning the soccer championship this summer, and I know you wanted to build that walkway for your treehouse thing—"

"You heard about that?" I interrupted.

"I hear things, kid. I'm not stupid," Mom laughed. "I know you had all sorts of other big plans. And I know you're going to miss your friends."

"Yeah, and I know what you're gonna say," I said quickly. "That I'll make all sorts of new, great friends in California and that I'll just have a great time and all and that everything will be great . . ."

"Actually, I wasn't going to say that, because you know all that already," Mom answered reasonably. "I know you'll find new friends right away. I'm not worried about that at all."

"Then what are you up here for?" I asked irritably.

Mom didn't answer right away. She looked at me for a few long seconds. "I came up here to make sure you were OK with all of this, with Mark and with the move to California."

"And if I wasn't?"

"Well, I don't know, really. I guess we'd just have to figure something out."

"Yeah, like I have a choice here," I mumbled.

"I know, Josh," Mom said sympathetically. "I know it's hard, being told what to do, that you have to move to a new place and that you have a new dad. But you really will like where we're going, and you *do* like Mark a lot. I know you do."

I looked up quickly. "I don't have to call him Dad if I don't want to, do I? You're not gonna make me do that, are you?"

"Not if you don't want to, Josh," Mom said qui-

30

etly. "That's your choice entirely. I'll leave it up to you."

"So I can just keep calling him Mark, if I want to?"

"If you want to."

I nodded. "OK, that's cool, I guess."

"Is there anything special we can do once we get to California? Anything fun you've thought about?"

"I guess Disney World is probably out now," I grumbled. "No way we're comin' all the way back across the country just to go there, I'll bet."

A funny smile played across my mom's face. "You know, Josh, it's amazing about things like that. Yes, you're right, it probably doesn't make sense to come clear across the country to go to Disney World in Florida. But don't you know that they have a Disneyland in California?"

"Can we go? For real?"

"Yes, for real," Mom laughed. "And because I won't have to look for a new job right away, we can spend two weeks there if you want, not just one."

I let out a *whoop* and hopped up off the floor. I gave her a high-five and bolted out of the room. Now, *this* was something I could talk about.

Maybe one of my friends had been there before and could help me figure out what I absolutely had to do there. There was work to be done before we moved to California.

△
CHAPTER 6

△How many times can you ride something before you decide you don't want to see it again for the rest of your life? I think I know. I think I found my limit. It's forty-seven times.

That's how many times I rode Big Thunder Mountain Railroad in Disneyland before I decided that I never wanted to ride it again. Well, at least not for a few weeks. I knew every inch of the track by heart. Every turn, every character along the ride, every hill.

I figured out *exactly* what time of day to wait in line so that you didn't have to sit there forever. First thing in the morning, when the park opens, is great. Lunchtime isn't too bad. But the hour before the park closes is the best. You can usually get two rides in then. Sometimes three, if you run.

It was funny. Every time, Mom would warn me not to hold my hands up high around the curves and down the hills because they had these little people who hid in the darkness and caught you doing it. And every time, I held my hands up high while Mom cowered in the seat beside me.

Mom was great, though. She basically let me do whatever I wanted for two whole weeks. We had hot dogs for breakfast and ice cream for lunch. Then we'd wait and go to McDonald's or Burger King when the park closed at night.

We didn't talk much for those two weeks. But it was all right. We didn't really have to. I knew what Mom was thinking. She wanted me to like Mark, to like California, to like what we were doing. But she didn't want to order me to do it.

Mom was like that. She never really told me what to do. She sort of talked me into it, like it was my idea or something.

Toward the end of the two weeks, we stopped running around to the rides frantically and waiting in line. We started hunting for the places that didn't have lines, where you could just listen to a band for a little while or watch something.

We discovered that, if you avoid the places where the whole entire universe absolutely, positively *has* to visit because they've seen it in all the travel brochures, you can actually have fun. You're sort of there, but not there. Part of the crowd, but off to the side, where the crowd isn't looking.

We packed up the house before we left for California and Disneyland. Mom and I flew out by ourselves. Mark was going to come out later, after the movers had cleared out our house. He was actually going to start his new job as a ranger while we were at Disneyland.

Most of the rangers, it turned out, lived in a small community in the national park. Mark said there were rows of cabins, and that all the rangers hung out together.

But if you were married, he said, you could choose to live in the town nearby. That's what we were going to do. Mom wanted me to live in a town where there were other kids, and where I wouldn't have to ride a bus forever to get to school.

Mark and I hadn't spent a whole lot of time together after the wedding. He just kind of moved into our house, got up in the morning, read the paper at the kitchen table, and then went to work down at the Interior Department, where he was taking these orientation classes for his new job.

I wasn't sure, exactly, what it was he was doing at his new job. He wore this green uniform with a patch on the sleeve that said he was a ranger with the National Park Service. He kept his black boots polished, like he was in the military or something.

Mark didn't tell us much about the classes he was attending, other than that he had to sit in these classrooms all day long and study things about trees and plants and forest fires and conservation and bear management and stream pollution.

When Mark came home at night, he usually watched a little TV with us. He read a book on the couch. We didn't talk. We were just there, together. I didn't look at him much. Mostly I did my own thing.

35

I could see why Mom liked Mark. He was a lot like Dad. That's what made me a little crazy inside. I didn't want him to be like Dad. I wanted him to be totally different.

I didn't want to forget Dad. I liked remembering things about him. I liked remembering the times when he'd sneak into my room after I was supposed to be asleep, close the door, and talk about junk with me until Mom would discover us and yell at Dad.

I liked remembering how he'd sit there with me for hours building something with me, patiently figuring out where every piece went long after I'd given up.

I liked remembering how he'd bought me a baseball mitt and worn it around the house for weeks to break it in. He'd sit on it in the chair while he watched TV, or bring it with him to the breakfast table and fiddle with it before work. By the time he finally handed it over to me, it was creased in all the right places and easy to hold.

I liked remembering how *angry* I'd been because my stupid soccer coach wouldn't let me play forward. He made me hang out on defense, near our own goal, while most of the other kids on the team got to score goals. Dad and I practiced how I'd take a ball and dribble it all the way up the field so I could shoot and score. I finally got my first goal, and when the coach yelled at me, Dad yelled right back at him. Nose to nose.

I liked remembering the way he taught me how to do wheelies on my new bike, how to hold the front wheel up without falling over backward. He showed me how to rock back and forth on the pedals to keep my balance.

I liked remembering the football games we played at dinner. Dad would fold a piece of paper into a triangle and then we'd push it back and forth across the table, ignoring Mom's scowl. Dad *loved* to kick field goals that smacked into the wall, because he knew how Mom would yell when he did it.

"You're putting nicks and marks in the wall!" Mom would yell.

"Oh, calm down, it's just a harmless piece of paper," Dad would answer soothingly, winking at me with one eye, making sure Mom didn't catch him in the act.

I didn't want Mark to be anything like Dad. I didn't want him to do anything the way Dad did. I just didn't.

On our last day at Disneyland, we didn't go on a single ride. Instead, we just walked around the park eating soft pretzels with tons of mustard on them.

We talked to one of the guys who walked on stilts in the parade every afternoon. The guy wanted to be an actor. He came out to California to be one of those actors in one of those shows on television that everyone knows and talks about. He wanted to be famous. Instead, at least for right now, he wandered around a park every afternoon in a clown suit, ten feet above everyone else in the crowd.

Mom managed to strike up a conversation with Mickey Mouse. What was it like, she asked him, to wear that huge, black, plastic head around all day? Hard, heavy, and sweaty, he answered. You could just barely see where you were going and little kids were constantly trying to rip your clothes off as a souvenir.

I spent twenty minutes studying the line that led into Splash Mountain. I finally figured out how it worked, but it wasn't easy. You see, Disneyland does this crazy thing. They make the lines wander all over the place so that you can never figure out *exactly* where you are or how close you are to actually getting onto the ride.

They must build it that way to keep people from freaking out right in the middle of their wait. You just shuffle along until, eventually, you arrive. You go forward, back, to the left, then the right, then across and around and back and left and back and around and right and forward and, well, then you're there.

Mom stood outside Goofy's "house" pretending she was a tour guide. She got about twenty kids listening to her describe what Goofy was doing inside the house. She told them she was Goofy's maid. They believed her.

I got one of the wandering clowns to teach me how to juggle. Actually, he didn't teach me. He showed me how *he* did it, then I tried it. And failed miserably. But I could see how it was done. You had to throw the balls up at an equal height, and keep throwing them up from one hand to the next without breaking the rhythm.

Mom and I stood off to the side at one of the big merchandise stands and tried to figure out how much Disneyland made off of tourists like Mom and me. They made a fortune, we finally decided. If you figure that they sold one trinket worth about $10 every 30 seconds, that was maybe $1,000 every hour. They had *hundreds* of those stands around the park, which meant they were raking in big, big money. I told Mom I wanted to be a concession-stand-person when I grew up. At first she thought that was silly, but I think she changed her mind.

There was a big mirror outside one of the restaurants. We stopped at it for a while and just watched what happened as people walked by. It was weird. When the big, fat guys would walk by, they'd stop, stare at the mirror, hitch up their pants so that the belt would ride up over their rolls of fat, and then move on. The women would peer into it, pat their hair, and straighten their blouses. The kids all made faces at it or giggled at themselves. The moms and dads all ignored it because they were too tired.

I was glad to leave Disneyland. I'd had enough. By the last day, I was ready to move to our new house somewhere in the High Sierras. I had no idea what it would be like to live in the mountains away from a big city, where I didn't know a soul and where I couldn't recognize a single thing.

But I was as ready as I'd ever be. It was time to move on.

CHAPTER 7

△You could see the mountains from a long way off. The snow-covered peaks jutted out sharply against the sky, which somehow seemed a little bluer here than in Washington.

I stared at them for the longest time as Mom and I drove up the interstate toward our new home. I didn't say much during the drive. I mostly looked out the window at the landscape.

There was no way around it. The mountains were *huge*. Absolutely huge, compared to what I was used to. It had been a few years since I'd seen mountains this size, and I guess I'd forgotten.

The Sierra Nevadas. Mom said there were some people who almost worshiped them, like they were God or something. "It's their sacred Holy Land," she told me. "There are some people who would practically kill to preserve them."

"What do you think about them?" I'd asked.

"They're just mountains," Mom had answered, smiling. "Pretty, big, and nice. But just mountains."

"But aren't we supposed to, like, protect them and stuff like that?"

"Yes, we are. God gave us charge over the Earth and the animals in it," Mom had said with a seriousness that surprised me. "But it is *wrong* to worship nature. Absolutely wrong."

"Worship it?"

"Treat it like it was God. There is only one, true God, and He made nature. You shouldn't worship His creation. You just take care of it."

Some of the highest peaks were three times the size of the mountains in the Appalachians I was used to. In the wintertime, Mom said, the passes through these highest peaks were closed because of the snowfall.

Mark had been living in the ranger camp while Mom and I were at Disneyland. That's where we were headed now. We were going to spend the night at the cabin he'd been staying at temporarily, and we were going to strike out for the town nearby first thing in the morning to look for a new house.

Mom had decided to let me look for a house with them. I'm not sure why. Maybe she thought it would help me feel better about what we were doing.

We left the interstate and turned onto a state road that led back into the High Sierra National Forest. I wasn't paying too much attention to where we were. We were about two hours north of Los Angeles, along the eastern side of California, but that was about as much as I knew.

There wasn't much to see as we drove along the road that wound its way slightly upward through the forest—just an endless panorama of trees, interspersed with shrubs and rocks. I thought I caught a glimpse of a deer a couple of times.

I spotted the sign to the ranger camp before Mom. It wasn't marked very well. It was just a small wooden sign on top of a stake pounded into the ground at the side of a dirt road that led off the main state road.

The words RANGER STATION #3 were carved into the wooden sign. The end of the sign was shaped like an arrow, pointing to the right off the paved road.

"There it is!" I shouted.

Mom blinked. "Don't shout," she answered, squinting to see what I was pointing to.

"The dirt road," I said, pointing.

Mom slowed the car. She spotted the sign and switched her right turn signal on. I never understood why people put their turn signals on out in the middle of nowhere where no one would see it. Habit, I guess.

"It *was* number three, right?" Mom asked me.

I shrugged. "I think so. But aren't you supposed to know that?"

"Just checking to see if you remembered."

"Hmmm," I grunted. "You forgot."

"No, no, I didn't."

I started laughing. "Boy, I can just see it. We never find Mark and we wander around for days inside the

43

national forest. We just sort of go from ranger camp to ranger camp, looking for him."

"Oh, stop. This is it. I remember now."

Mom turned off onto the dirt road and began to drive slowly along it. There were no posted speed limits, but that wasn't necessary, really. If you went faster than fifteen miles an hour, you sort of wiped out the bottom of your car.

We drove along for about a mile, with heavy woods on either side of the car. Then we emerged into a clearing of sorts. A road with big truck-tire tracks crossed the road here, going off to the left.

Mom stopped the car. We both followed the tire tracks with our eyes. We stared at the sight where they led to for a long time.

An entire part of the forest had just been, well, kind of *obliterated*. It was as if some fantastically huge giant had stopped here, taken a huge swipe with a big sword, and lopped off hundreds of trees in one fell swoop.

Most of the trees still lay on their side. The trucks had not come yet to pick them all up and cart them off. The area where the trees had been cut was huge, maybe the size of a few big football stadiums. It ran up the side of a small mountain slope we could see clearly from the car.

"What is that?" I asked finally.

"A clearcut."

"A what?"

"It's a style of logging," Mom said somberly. "It's where the timber company comes in and just takes down every tree they can find, almost for as far as the eye can see."

44

"They can do that?"

Her eyebrows arched a little. "Not right now, they can't. At least not in the national forests of the Sierra Nevadas for the next couple of years, Mark says."

"But isn't this the national forest?"

"It is." Mom nodded. "But they didn't change the rules until just recently. This was probably done before they changed them."

"So why'd they change the rules?"

"To protect the spotted owl."

"The spotted owl? What's that?"

"An owl with spots!" Mom grinned.

I groaned. "Real funny."

Mom started to ease the car forward. I was glad to leave the place. I had no idea whether it was right or wrong to do what they'd done to the forest here. I didn't know what "clearcutting" was, exactly. But it *looked* painful, like someone had just scarred a beautiful thing.

Two miles later, we reached the outskirts of Ranger Station #3. As Mark had told us, it was nothing more than a row of simple, rustic cabins about a hundred feet or so off the dirt road.

I imagined that the place was usually pretty quiet and serene back here in the heart of the forest, with nothing more than trees and rocks and shrubs on all sides.

But something was clearly wrong today. There were rangers in their dark green outfits running in and out of cabins and back and forth from one cabin to the next as we drove up. They were obviously frantic about something. Everyone ignored us.

45

"What's goin' on, do you think?" I asked.

"Maybe a forest fire. I don't know. Let's go find Mark and see."

Mom brought the car to a stop slowly in front of one of the cabins. It was hard to tell which one Mark might be in. They all looked exactly alike. We hopped out. Mom looked over at me.

"Who do we ask?" she called to me.

"Beats me."

We stood there like that for a couple of minutes. The rangers were still running back and forth. Off in the distance, I thought I could hear the faint sound of something. *Whop-whop-whop*, it went. I cocked an ear to hear it better.

An instant later, the leaves started to blow furiously around us. A sharp wind whipped up, tossing dirt in our faces. I blinked rapidly. The *whop-whop* sound was quite close now. I looked up, shielding my eyes.

A dark green helicopter hurtled across the sky, just above the tops of the trees. It roared into view, its nose tilted down slightly as it sped forward.

The helicopter slowed as it came in over the clearing where the cabins were all situated. It began to hover over a clear patch. Dirt and leaves started to whirl around like little tornadoes beneath it.

As the helicopter touched down, several rangers ran out of a cabin about fifty feet away and started to sprint toward it. One of them was Mark.

"Mark!" Mom yelled.

Mark stopped and turned toward us. He shaded his eyes to keep the dirt and debris out of his eyes.

He spotted us and waved. He yelled something to the other rangers and then ran toward us.

"What's goin' on?" I shouted at Mark when he was almost to us.

"A bear mauling!" Mark shouted back. "Or at least we think so. That's what the chopper saw from the sky. He couldn't land, so he called it in."

Mark gave my Mom a quick hug. I looked away, toward the helicopter just as it shut down. The blades slowed and then stopped. One ranger emerged from it and began to jog back toward the cabins with the others.

"So what now?" Mom asked in a normal voice. Now that the helicopter had shut down, it seemed unnaturally quiet.

"Yeah, why isn't it out there helping the people?" I asked Mark.

"We don't know there were people out there," Mark answered. "Not yet. The pilot only saw the campsite from the sky."

"So how will you . . . ?"

"We'll take the Land Rovers," Mark said quickly. "Come with me. You can listen in on the debriefing with the topo maps in the main cabin."

"Topo maps?" I asked blankly.

"You'll see." Mark smiled. "Come on. We'll be late."

△
CHAPTER 8

△The moment Mark, Mom, and I walked through the cabin door, one of the rangers looked up sharply. He was older than the others. His hair was starting to gray around the fringes. He glared at Mom and me, and then at Mark. "We can't have civilians in here!" he barked.

"This is my wife, Casey, sir, and my . . . my stepson, Joshua," Mark stuttered. "They, uh, aren't exactly civilians."

The ranger continued to glare at Mark, but then, without another word looked back at the maps spread out on a table in the cabin. Mark motioned for us to stand off to one side quietly.

I tried to peer through the crowd of rangers around the table. I could catch glimpses of what looked like maps with big circles and rivers on it. They were green and black. I wasn't sure what kind they were.

"Here," said one of the rangers. He stabbed a finger at a spot on the map.

"In Redstone Canyon?" one of the rangers said. "You're sure?"

"Yep," the first ranger said. "That's where I saw the campsite."

"But we haven't heard of any bears there. Not in a long while," said the second ranger.

"And it's so far from anything," said a third. "If it's a bear that's gotten used to the garbage and food from tourists in Yosemite, what would it be doing way down in Redstone?"

"I'm telling you, the site was in Redstone," said the first, who was obviously the helicopter pilot.

"Tell us what you saw," said the ranger who'd challenged Mark when we'd come in. It was obvious to me he was in charge here.

The pilot pointed at the map again. I edged closer to the table for a better view. "I came over the canyon wall," he said, "and the campsite was at the base. They must have been climbing the face of the wall."

"Did you see them?"

The pilot shook his head. "I used the binocs for several minutes. There was no sign of them, at least not in the camp."

"What about on the canyon wall?"

"Nope," the pilot said. "I looked it over pretty carefully. No ropes or pitons or anything. There was no sign of them anywhere."

"How many people do you think?" asked the ranger who was in charge.

"I spotted three tents," the pilot said.

"And they were torn up pretty bad?"

The pilot nodded. "The site was a mess. The tents were torn to shreds, and the provisions were scattered around in maybe a fifty-foot radius. The bear had taken the place apart."

The ranger in charge nodded. "All right. Any suggestions on how we get there?"

"The Land Rovers?" Mark suggested. (Somewhat timidly, I thought.)

"Too far," said a ranger. "It would take us an hour or so through some rough terrain."

The ranger in charge turned to the pilot. "You can't get into the canyon?"

"Too narrow," the pilot said grimly. "It was all I could do to hover over it briefly."

"The top of the canyon wall. Can you take us there, hover over it for a few minutes and then come back to pick us up when I radio?"

"Sure," the pilot said. "No problem with that."

"Then we'll take ropes and go down the wall," the ranger in charge ordered. "We'll take the rope ladder down from the chopper, and then scale the wall." He looked around the room. "Jennings and Samuels. You can ride with me. Go grab the ropes and equipment."

Two rangers turned sharply and sprinted from the room. The others turned back to the maps spread out on the table.

"Can I go?" I suddenly asked. It just sort of popped out. I was dying to go see this, and I just asked before I knew why. Had I thought about it, I would have kept my big mouth shut.

"What was that?" the ranger in charge asked, looking around at me.

"Josh!" Mark said, a slight edge of fear in his voice.

"It was me," I said, ignoring Mark for the moment. "And I asked if I could go."

The ranger in charge gave me a hard look and then turned to Mark. "You said this was your stepson?"

Mark nodded.

The ranger looked at Mark, then at me, then over at the pilot. "The chopper carry the extra weight?"

The pilot shrugged. "Plenty to spare."

I looked over at Mom. Her face was white as a sheet. I *knew* she didn't like this, not at all. But she looked at Mark for help. "He'll be fine," Mark whispered. "The helicopter will hover and wait while they take a look at the campsite."

"But . . . but is it safe?" Mom asked him in a forced whisper.

Mark nodded. "Yes, it's safe."

"So can I go?" I asked, still wondering where in the world this newfound courage and boldness had come from. Or perhaps foolishness.

The ranger in charge frowned for what seemed like the longest time. This was easily well beyond what the ranger manual probably said about proper procedure. But something kept him from just saying no right away. I wondered vaguely what it was.

"All right with you, ma'am?" the ranger asked my mom finally.

She balked for a moment, and then nodded slowly. "Yes, I suppose. As long as he'll be safe."

"He'll be fine, ma'am," the ranger said. "He can

ride in the back, with the gear. He'll be in good hands." The ranger looked over at Mark, and an ironic smile creased his face. "You got your hands full with that one, Rawlings," he told Mark, inclining his head in my direction.

Mark smiled for the first time since we'd arrived. "I think I can see that."

Mom turned to me. "What in the world were you thinking?" she whispered.

"I wanted to see," I offered lamely.

Mom sighed. "Well, you've done it now. I suppose there's no turning back."

"Aw, Mom, I'll be OK. The ranger said."

"Well, young man, you do *exactly* as they tell you," she said sternly. "You hear me?"

"All right, I hear you."

"Promise?"

"I promise. I won't move unless they tell me to."

Mark leaned close. "Just do whatever Mr. Wilson tells you."

"He's the guy in charge?" I asked.

Mark nodded. "Joe Wilson. He's been here for nearly twenty years. He's a legend in these parts. He knows every inch of the wilderness, they say."

I looked back at him. I understood, a little, why Mark was afraid of him. I was too.

Jennings poked his head back through the door a second later. "Ropes and gear secured in the helicopter, sir," he called to Mr. Wilson.

"Great," Mr. Wilson responded. "Then let's roll." He looked over at me. "What's your first name, Rawlings?"

"Joshua," I answered, trying to keep the quiver of

fear out of my voice. "And, um, my last name, it's Landis."

Mr. Wilson glanced over at Mark, a funny look in his eyes. But it passed quickly, and he turned back to me. "Well, Landis, move it! No time to waste."

I jerked to attention and hustled over to Mr. Wilson's side. I gave Mom and Mark a timid wave and then followed the rangers over to the helicopter.

I stayed a couple of steps behind Mr. Wilson. I climbed through the door.

"Back there," Mr. Wilson said, pointing at a pile of ropes and other gear stowed at the back of the helicopter. I clambered to the back and sat awkwardly on the ropes. I pressed my nose against the window to look out.

A moment later we were airborne. There was no turning back now.

△
CHAPTER 9

△ I didn't say anything for about the first five minutes of the trip. I just listened to the talk among the four rangers inside the big helicopter. It was cramped, hot, and stuffy at the back of the helicopter, but I wasn't about to complain.

Mr. Wilson was clearly in charge. The other rangers hung on his every word, nodding every so often at something he said. They only spoke, really, when they were called on.

Mr. Wilson spoke with a soft intensity and conviction about their mission that told me he'd done this kind of thing before.

As we flew, I looked more closely at the rangers I was now riding with. The two rangers Mr. Wilson had picked for this job were both much younger

55

than him. They looked like they were just out of college.

Mike Jennings was tall and rangy. Parts of his short brown hair stuck up in tufts around his head. His shirt was slightly wrinkled and the tail was almost hanging out of the back of his pants. His black tie wasn't knotted well. His shoes were scuffed in several spots and one shoelace was broken and re-tied in three places.

Lee Samuels was a few inches shorter than Jennings. I couldn't tell what color his hair was, because it was cropped so close. I guessed it was probably sandy blond, but I couldn't be sure. His shirt was buttoned at the top, and his tie was pulled up snug. His shirt was pulled so tight across his chest, I wondered if it wasn't a size too small.

The pilot, John Littlehorse, was an Indian. Or at least I figured he had to be. I wasn't sure. I'd have to remember to ask Mark later. His shiny black hair was pulled back into a neat ponytail. He wore some kind of a turquoise necklace, and he had a gold earring in his left ear.

Mr. Wilson was a stark contrast to all three. He was shorter than all of them, but his back was so ramrod straight you didn't notice. His shirt was stiff, the sleeves wrinkle-free. His tie was clipped to his shirt neatly. His pants were creased. I noticed that his black boots were spit-polished, not a scuff on them.

None of them paid even the slightest bit of attention to me as we raced over the tops of trees, banked around a tall, snow-capped mountain peak and down into a valley. Which was fine by me. I just wanted to watch.

I was torn between listening to Mr. Wilson explain the mission and looking out the window at the wilderness spinning by beneath me. In the end, I pressed my face against the window and kept half an ear to their conversation.

A large stream cascaded down the side of the mountain peak we'd just skirted. It worked its way down the side of the mountain and eventually became an even larger stream that fed into a lake at the bottom of the valley.

A sea of trees extended for as far as the eye could see. There seemed no end to the wilderness, not even from the sky. Only mountain peaks broke the landscape to the north of where we were.

John banked the helicopter and headed directly toward another peak in the distance. It took us several minutes to reach it.

As we drew closer, I could see the sheer rock face. This had to be Redstone Canyon. The campsite had to be at the bottom of the cliff.

"OK, bring it in slow, John," Mr. Wilson ordered.

"Yes, sir," the pilot answered.

Mr. Wilson turned toward me. "Kid, make yourself useful. Start handing me the ropes. Don't tangle them."

I moved off the ropes and began to hand them forward. Mike took them from me and set them down next to the door. Then I handed him a bag that jangled from the pitons inside. Finally, I handed over the rope ladder stowed at the back.

"Good job, kid," Mr. Wilson said without smiling. "You've earned your pay. Now, while we're down there, just watch. Do *not* come anywhere near the door. You can watch out the window. Got it?"

"Got it," I squeaked.

The helicopter slowed and began to hover. I looked down. I could see the campsite. Sure enough, there was debris everywhere, scattered in all directions around what had previously been a tight circle of three tents.

The tents were now in tatters. There was almost nothing left intact in the rest of the camp. Bits and scraps of paper had blown off in one direction and were stuck in leaves and branches about fifty feet or so from the campsite.

The canyon wall was straight up and down. You clearly had to know what you were doing to get up that thing. It was no place for beginning rock climbers.

When the helicopter was hovering nearly motionless over the top of the canyon wall, Mr. Wilson attached the rope ladder to two metal rings and then pushed the door open. He threw the ladder out and it whipped down, nearly touching the ground.

Next, all three rangers tossed out the ropes and piton bag I'd handed forward. Mr. Wilson clipped a portable radio to his belt. Without another word, all three of them climbed through the door and down the rope ladder.

When all three were secure on the ground, Mike gave a tug on the ladder. John turned to me. "Can you pull it up, kid?"

"Me?"

"Yeah, you!" John smiled. "Don't worry. It won't bite."

"But Mr. Wilson said not to get near the door . . . ?"

John reached over and jerked on the rope ladder from the top. Part of it came clattering into the helicopter. "There," he said. "Now you can pull it in without getting near the door."

I moved forward and began to pull the ladder in. I piled it onto one of the seats.

"Why don't you come up here?" John said. "You can sit with me in the co-pilot's chair and watch."

"Really?"

"Really. It's all right. We won't tell ol' Wilson."

I ducked my head and eased my way forward. I slid into the seat and stared out the big bubble window that formed the front of the helicopter.

All three of them were securing the ropes at the top of the canyon wall with a handful of pitons. They were all pounding away furiously, with a practiced ease that told me they'd done this kind of thing a lot.

They quickly looped their ropes through, knotted them, and then stood up. They tied one end to their waists and moved to the edge of the cliff wall.

"We'll wait until they're down safely before we move on," John whispered.

I wondered why he was whispering, but I didn't say anything.

John moved the throttle forward slightly, and the helicopter rotated forward a little so we could look directly at the rock wall as they went down.

All three climbed over the edge, holding the ropes

firmly. They took two or three small steps to get their bearings and then just sort of jumped off into space.

They pushed off with their legs, thrusting their bodies out and then letting the rope slide through their hands. Then they gripped the ropes hard and came back to the wall. They hit and immediately sprang outward again.

Mike and Lee were fast. They took huge leaps outward and came hurtling back to the canyon wall so rapidly I thought sure they'd crash. But their legs were obviously tough enough to absorb the shock at impact, because they didn't falter at all.

Mr. Wilson took shorter leaps, but he was nearly as fast as the two of them. Where Mike and Lee almost radiated with raw energy and talent, Mr. Wilson had a skill and flair that told me he'd been doing this for years and years.

"Man, they're good," I said in hushed awe.

"Some of the best rock climbers on the coast," John answered. "I'd match 'em with anyone."

"Even Mr. Wilson?"

He laughed. *"Especially* Mr. Wilson."

When they reached the bottom, John began to ease the throttle forward and left. We gradually eased away from the cliff wall and then flew off.

"What now?" I asked.

"We wait," John said. "There's a place to land further down the canyon, maybe a thousand yards from here. The old man'll radio in when they're finished."

John brought the helicopter down a few seconds

later, in a clearing alongside a creekbed. The radio crackled just as we were landing.

"John? You there?" came Mr. Wilson's voice.

John grabbed the mike and flipped a switch. "Roger. I can hear you fine. What's the scene like? Over."

"Good news. No sign of life, and no indication that anyone was dragged off, either. Over."

"Great. Call when you're ready for pickup. Over."

"Will do. Over."

John switched off the microphone. "Boy, that's great. Maybe they weren't there when the bear showed up."

I nodded. "Yeah, that'd be cool."

We sat there in silence and waited. With the helicopter blades shut down, it was very, very quiet. Except for the wind, there were almost no sounds to break the quiet.

"So what kind of a bear do you think it was?" I finally asked.

"Most likely a black," John said. "I doubt one of the brown bears would come down this way."

"Not a grizzly?"

John shook his head. "Nope. Can't possibly be a grizzly. We haven't had any grizzlies here in these parts for a long time."

"Really?"

"Yep. Really. My people have stories, of course, about grizzlies in the High Sierras around here. From before. Years ago, I mean. But not anymore."

"I guess I just thought . . ."

"Yeah, most people do." John nodded. "They think they'll find grizzlies all over the West. But

61

grizzlies have been hounded, shot, tracked down, and killed so much that there aren't many of them around anymore. And there aren't any in this part of the Sierra Nevadas. You might find a few in the highest parts way north of here."

"Not even one?"

"Oh, there are a couple of old coot stories about grizzlies in the deep wilderness around here, well away from man. But they're just stories. Ain't no grizzlies around here. Period. I'd bet my pay this week it was a black bear that scattered that camp."

I leaned back in my chair. I could see I had a lot to learn.

The radio crackled again. "John Littlehorse. This is Base Three. Can you copy? Over?"

John reached over to the console and flipped another switch, probably to a different frequency. "Yes, I copy. We're at the campsite. No sign that the bear got anyone. Over."

"Yes, we know," the voice said. "The people who were at the site just turned up at a ranger outpost north of you. They left the site a day ago and hiked north. Over."

John pumped the air with a fist. "All *right*. That's great news. I'll let the guys here know. Thanks. Over."

"We'll send a clean-up crew out in a Rover. You guys can come back anytime you want. Over."

John nodded. "Thanks. Be back shortly. Over." He reached over and flipped the console switch back. "Wilson. This is Littlehorse. Come in. Over."

"Wilson here. What's up? Over."

"They found your hikers. They went north, and

62

just turned up at a ranger outpost north of here. We can head home now. Clean-up crew's on its way. Over."

"Fine. Give us five more minutes to canvass the area completely, and then fly in. Over."

Five minutes later, we were back over the site. All three had begun to climb back up the ropes when we arrived. It didn't take them long to scale the wall. They just basically walked straight up the wall, hand over hand.

I tossed the rope ladder out the door just as they reached the top. Then I scurried to my post in the back of the helicopter.

Minutes later, we were racing back toward Ranger Station #3. I couldn't wait to tell somebody—*any-body*—about the whole deal.

△
CHAPTER 10

△"Mom, it was just so *cool*. I mean, they just jumped out into space and sailed right down the wall. It was, like, three or four big, huge jumps and they were down the wall."

Mom listened to me patiently as we drove away from the ranger station, toward a small town nearby called Jupiter. I was out of my seatbelt, leaning forward through the opening of the two front seats in the car.

"You need to buckle up, Josh," she ordered quietly.

"Yeah, I know. I will, in just a sec."

"No, now. We'll be on the road soon."

I sighed and leaned back. I snapped the seatbelt on and then strained forward again. "Mark, is it true there aren't any grizzlies in the mountains around here?"

Mark nodded. "That's what I'm told. It's what all the books say about this part of the Sierra Nevadas."

"How come?"

"Oh, we're probably too close to bigger cities. Once, there were a whole bunch of grizzlies in the High Sierras, here included. But that was a while ago. The grizzly's been gone from the High Sierras around here for a long time."

I remembered what John Littlehorse had told me. "But there are stories about maybe a grizzly or two still left, way back in the wilderness?"

"Don't know." Mark shrugged. "If there are, I haven't heard 'em. But I've only been here a few weeks." He turned in his seat briefly, looked at me, and then turned back to keep his eyes on the road. "If you're interested, I'll ask around, though."

"I'm interested," I said quickly.

"Done, then. I'll see what people know."

I sat back in my seat and looked out the window again. We came to the end of the dirt road and turned right. Mark stepped on the gas and the car lurched forward.

"You been to Jupiter?" I asked Mark.

"A little," he answered.

"What's it like?"

Mark pursed his lips. "Oh, I don't know. It's a small town, maybe five thousand people to it. Not anything like what you're used to in D.C. You can zip from one end to the other in a flash, no problem. No such thing as rush hour in Jupiter, that's for sure."

"Been to the junior high?"

Mark nodded. "I have, as a matter of fact. It's out

66

west of the town, at the base of one of the mountains. There's a river that runs out back of the school, and the Rocky Gorge cliffs aren't too far away. In fact, you can see them from some of the classrooms, I'll bet."

"Rocky Gorge. What's that?"

"It's where you'll probably learn how to rock climb, I'll wager. If you want to, that is. They have handholds up the side, and it isn't a sheer face."

"Oh, yeah, I want to. No question."

"That's what I figured!" Mark laughed.

"So how big's the school?"

"Hm. Good question. I'll bet there were maybe fifteen or twenty classrooms. What's that work out to, maybe a few hundred kids in the school?"

I wasn't great at math, but that seemed about right. Even at that, it would still be a whole lot smaller than my own school in Washington.

I'd promised Mom that I'd try to be good about all of this. And, man, I was trying. I was. But it wasn't easy. Some part of me still hoped against all hope that Mark would suddenly just yank the wheel of the car to the right and head back to Washington.

But I knew it wasn't about to happen. We were here to stay, and I'd just have to live with it.

My heart fell as we began to enter Jupiter. Small doesn't even begin to describe it. It was a hole in the wall. The main street was one long strip, with houses and buildings almost touching each other on either side of the street.

There was the Jupiter Gas and Groceries. There was a Jupiter Diner. There was a Jupiter Hardware, a Jupiter Drugs, and a Jupiter Five and Dime. Oh, yeah, and a Jupiter Sporting Goods, which mostly had a bunch of guns and deer antlers in the window.

I closed my eyes and talked to God, which I did by myself every so often when I was really lonely, or when I was down or angry. I was pretty sure God was listening. Not absolutely, positively, 100 percent certain. But pretty sure.

Why am I here? I like D.C. I like all my friends there. Most of us were going to the same junior high, and the summer was going to be great. So why am I stuck out here in Jupiter, with all the hicks and cornballs?

Yeah, the mountains are OK. All right, they are more than OK. They are awesome. It was cool the way the rangers went down that rock face to the campsite.

But Jupiter? It is depressing. It is like my worst nightmare of a place I never want to visit, and now I have to live here.

But the mountains, yeah, and the lakes formed by the rivers running down the sides of some of the peaks, and the deep wilderness where only a few people have visited, and the miles and miles of trees. Those are interesting.

But I don't know anything about that kind of junk. I've been to the National Zoo and stared at a few of the animals through the bars. That's it. That's almost the complete, sum total of my brush with the wild.

Yeah, sure, I've been hiking with my dad. But it was a long time ago, before he died, and I don't remember a whole lot about it, other than the fact that the mosquitoes wiped me out.

So how do I do this? How do I figure all of this out, God? How do I make my peace with this? How do I do that?

"Mom!" I practically yelled.

"What?" Mom answered me, wincing a little.

"Can we, like, look for this *really* cool place to live? Not in Jupiter, but maybe near here? Back in the mountains or something like that?"

Mark and my mom stole a quick glance at each other. They'd been talking. I could see that.

"All right, give," I demanded. "What's up?"

"Well, Josh," Mom said slowly, "you know Mark was out here while we were at Disneyland . . ." Her voice trailed off.

I got it. Mark had found something already. But a slight panic hit me. "You haven't actually bought anything yet, have you?"

"No, no, of course not, Josh," Mark said quickly. "We would never do that. The furniture's in storage. This is going to be your home, too. We want to make sure you like it. But I think you will."

"Where is it?" I asked, my voice squeaking a little.

"It's northeast of Jupiter, maybe two miles out of town," Mark said. "It's set into the side of a small mountain, facing east. It has solar panels to catch the sun. And it's high enough on the mountain that you can look down on the valley below."

"And I'll bet there isn't anybody around for miles," I said glumly. "We're probably out in the middle of nowhere and I'll have to take a bus or something to find anybody to hang out with."

Mom and Mark looked at each other again. "Actually, Josh, Mark says there are other homes on the mountain," Mom said slowly. "He says there's a little community of families. Three of the ranger families are there, one up above and two below."

"Hmmm," I grunted. "Sounds kinda weird. It's not like one of those places where everybody lives together and shares all their junk, is it?"

"No," Mark laughed. "It's not a commune, if that's what you mean. It's just a small mountain overlooking a nice valley. A few families have built their homes there."

I looked out the window. Despite my very best efforts, a tiny, little spark of hope was beginning to flicker somewhere within me. I tried to put it out. But there it was. I decided to wait and see.

We left Jupiter and immediately began to climb into the hills north of the town. I spotted the mountain right away. You could see it quite clearly from the outskirts of Jupiter.

As we got to it, the road swerved to the right and down into the valley. Then we began to work our way back up the side of it, toward some houses that were, in fact, built into the side of the mountain.

I held my breath. God, please make it nice. Make it just like Mark said it was.

We passed two houses set back from the road, went through a deep overhang of trees, and then came to a dirt driveway on the right that led up higher on the mountain. Mark slowed and turned onto the drive.

We drove up it in silence. I still couldn't see the house. It was well off the road.

The driveway was lined by trees. I spotted a small

stream running alongside it on the left. I wondered vaguely where its source was.

I spotted the dark wood of the home through the leaves of the trees before we came to the end of the drive. It was a log cabin! And it was huge—much, much bigger than our home back in Washington.

There was a pond in front of the house. I could see a stream feeding into it. There were several big solar panels on the roof, like Mark had said.

As the car came to a stop at the end of the circular drive, I could see that the home was built out of real logs, with some white junk plastered neatly between each of them. There was a monstrous porch that seemed to go all the way around the house.

The back of the house just seemed to disappear into the side of the mountain. For all I knew, it went on forever, through to the other side.

The house had a big stone chimney and one solitary window up at the very top of the house, with a perfect view of the valley. I wondered what that place was. I just *had* to see it.

I had the car door open before we'd even come to a complete stop. I raced for the door of the house. Mom didn't try to stop me.

I didn't even think whether anyone was home or not. I just barged right through the front door and stood there, looking at the place.

The front hall was every bit as huge as you'd expect in a house this size, with a big wooden bench built right into the wall as you came in, and wooden pegs to hang your coats.

I could see the kitchen off to the left. It had about

a million windows in it. On my right, I spotted a very large fireplace built into a stone hearth.

But I ignored all this and headed straight for the wide, stone stairway that led to the second level. I noticed that it was cool in the house. It felt good.

There were several rooms on the second level. I ducked my head into them quickly and then looked around for the way up to the third level. I spotted it, finally. There was a sturdy wooden ladder at the back of the house. I clambered up it.

It led to a loft. There was a bunkbed built right into the side of the house that was under the mountain. I walked over to the window I'd seen from the driveway and peered out.

Mom spotted me and waved. I waved back, and then looked out. I could see the entire valley from here. I could see for miles and miles. The view was endless. Sunlight poured in through the window.

I felt a lump in my throat. This was my new room. I knew it, as surely as I'd known anything. It was my place.

I caught some movement below. Mom and Mark turned to look down the driveway. Mark waved at someone.

There was a girl pedaling a bike up the driveway. She was whipping her short black hair back and forth furiously as she raced up the driveway. I turned, ran to the ladder, and half-jumped, half-climbed down. I sprinted down the stone stairs and out the front door.

The girl skidded to a halt, kicking up a cloud of dirt as her rear tire took out a big patch of the driveway. She let the bike fall to the ground and walked over to me briskly.

We were exactly the same height, if I stood on my tiptoes just a little. She was wiry. She had a tan already, even though summer hadn't actually started. Her face was rugged and weather-beaten, like she'd been outdoors a lot.

"So you movin' in here or what?" she demanded.

"I dunno," I mumbled. "Who're you?"

"Ashley Deaton. What's your name?"

"Josh. Joshua Landis."

Ashley thrust a hand out. I took it. Ashley gave it a big strong shake. "Glad to meet ya, Josh. So are ya movin' in, or what?"

I looked over at Mom and Mark. Neither said anything. "Can we?" I asked them.

"Do you like it?" Mom asked softly.

I nodded, without hesitation. "It's great. There's a neat loft up top. Can that be my room?"

"If you like," Mom said.

I turned back to Ashley. "Yeah, it looks like we're movin' in. You live near here?"

Ashley turned and pointed back down the road. "Our house is the next one over," she said. "There's a cutback trail between the two houses. I'll show it to you, if you want."

"Can I?" I asked Mom.

Mom laughed. "Knock yourself out, Josh. Just don't get lost, or stay away too long. Come right back after you've visited Ashley's house, OK?"

"I'll bring him right back, Mrs. Landis," Ashley promised.

"My last name is Rawlings, Ashley," my mom

said, giving me a sideways glance. "I just remarried. Joshua goes by Landis."

"Oh, well, OK, Mrs., um, Mrs. Rawlings," Ashley said, giving me a funny look. "Anyway, I'll leave my bike here. I'll get it when we come back."

And we were off, on the way to a trail behind my new home in California.

△

CHAPTER 11

△ Ashley had been right. The cutback trail wound down straight to her house, which was also built directly into the side of the mountain. It took us about two minutes to get to her house.

Even though we'd run the whole way, Ashley wasn't even winded. "Come on," she said as her house came into view. "Let's race."

I tried to keep up with her. But I wasn't nearly as sure of my footing here as she was. I kept glancing down at the ground as I sprinted, just to make sure there wasn't a root or something that was about to trip me up.

Still, I managed to catch Ashley almost as we got to her front porch. We were neck and neck the last few feet. I surged. I was just about to overtake her, when my foot caught a rock and I lost my balance and went flying, face forward.

I hit the ground hard. All the breath went out of me. I just lay there for a second, dazed. Then I started to rub my hands, which were raw and sore from where they'd skidded on the ground as I'd caught my fall.

"You all right?" Ashley asked quickly, as she turned abruptly and moved over to my side.

"Yeah, I'm OK." I winced.

"You sure?"

"M' OK," I mumbled. I rolled over onto my back and stared up at the sky.

You know, it was weird. I could swear the sky was a different color. It was blue, all right. But it was a different kind of blue than the one I was used to in Washington, D.C. It was deeper, somehow. Or clearer, perhaps.

"Josh!" Ashley said sharply.

I shook my head and looked over. "What?"

"What were you doin'? You had this goofy smile on your face."

I rolled back over onto my stomach and pushed off the ground. Before Ashley could say anything, I took off for the front porch. I got there, touched the railing that surrounded it, and turned. "I win," I said, thrusting both hands high in victory.

"No way. I just stopped because you fell."

"Did you *actually* touch the front porch?"

"Well, um, no, but . . ."

"Then I win."

"That's crazy. There's no way."

"Sure there is. You gotta touch to win. Everybody knows that. It's like the law or somethin'."

"Where? What law?"

"You know. The law."

Ashley scowled. "No such law. You're just makin' it up 'cause I crunched you on the way here."

"Hey. I touched first. Period."

"So? You also did a major root pig, too."

"A *what*?"

"A root pig. You know, diggin' up dirt with your nose."

I laughed. That was funny. It didn't sound like California, though. "Where are you from, anyway?"

"Here. Waddya mean?"

"I mean, from before here. Before you moved here."

Ashley put her hands on her hips. "What's that supposed to mean?"

"It doesn't mean anything. I was just curious. You lived here for a while or not?"

Ashley shrugged. "Oh. Well, we moved here two years ago, from Ohio."

"So you're new here, too?"

"I guess. But I hardly remember Ohio much now. It's pretty cool out here."

"You *like* Jupiter?"

"Yeah, sure. There's all sorts of stuff to do around here."

"Like what?"

"Hike. Climb rocks. Go cavin', if you have a guide. Ski up on the big mountains, even in the spring sometimes. Camp in the summer. Follow the

Muir Trail up one of the big mountains. Swim in the big lake on the other side of this mountain. That enough?"

I suddenly remembered something Mark had mentioned. "Your dad. Is he a ranger, too?"

Ashley nodded. "Yeah, he is. That's why we moved. So?"

"Nothin'. It's just that my, uh . . . my new stepdad is a ranger, too."

"Which part of the forest?" she asked.

"Which part of the forest? Whatcha mean?"

"You know, is he near Sequoia, or Yosemite or High Sierra? Which part?"

I was confused. "He's in the High Sierra Park, I guess. That's where I was today."

Ashley gave me a strange look. "You mean, he works *in* the park?"

"Yeah, I guess."

"Like, he's part of the National Park Service? Does he wear a green uniform?"

"Yeah, he does. What's that mean?"

Ashley looked over at her house. "Nothin'. It's just that my dad is a forest ranger."

"There's a difference?"

Ashley nodded. "You'll see."

Ashley's mom came out on the porch just then, before I could ask her what the difference was. I guess I figured a ranger was a ranger.

Mrs. Deaton was wearing an apron, and her hair was up in a tight bun. She looked like she was a lot older than my mom. Her wire-rimmed glasses were perched on the end of her nose. She moved to the edge of the porch, drying her hands on a dish towel.

"Ashley, honey, who's this?" she called out.

"Josh! He just moved in up the mountain."

A happy smile lit up Mrs. Deaton's face. It made me smile, too. I couldn't help it. "In the big cabin house?" Mrs. Deaton asked.

"I think," I answered, as Ashley and I began to walk toward the front porch.

Mrs. Deaton's head started to bob up and down. "Well, that's just fine, real fine. Welcome, welcome, Josh. You'll like our little community of Ganymede here. Good people here."

I cast a sideways glance at Ashley, and then looked back at Mrs. Deaton. "Ganymede? I thought the town was named Jupiter."

Mrs. Deaton laughed. It was a full, rich laugh, with no hidden shadows and with nothing held back. "It is, it is. But Ganymede is our little community here on the mountain. Self-named and self-perpetuated, I should say."

I was thoroughly confused. "But . . ."

"Look it up when you get the chance," Mrs. Deaton said heartily. "Explore for yourself. Find the answer. It'll make sense."

"OK," I mumbled.

A big man suddenly came through the front door and strode across the porch in three steps. He wore a red-and-black checked flannel shirt, jeans, and soft-leather boots of some kind. He was in a hurry.

"Where you goin', Dad?" Ashley called out.

Mr. Deaton gave his wife a quick peck on the cheek and paused only long enough to answer his daughter. "Gotta run. Those fools in the Park Service think they found another park bear stirrin' up trouble."

"I know," I said quickly. "I just got back from the campsite."

Mr. Deaton stopped absolutely dead in his tracks. He turned slowly and looked at me squarely. I returned the gaze, but not without some trouble.

"What's that?" he asked finally.

"I said we were just at the campsite." My voice almost squeaked.

"And how's that, exactly? I hear the campsite's quite a ways from here," Mr. Deaton demanded, clearly not believing me.

"Well, um, you know, it doesn't take too long when you fly by helicopter."

Mr. Deaton's jaw clenched. He squeezed and unsqueezed his fists. "You mean they got those idiotic helicopters out already for something like this?"

"I dunno. I guess. I rode in one, I mean."

"And you flew to the campsite?" Mr. Deaton asked tightly.

Ashley moved close and whispered in my ear, "I tried to warn you."

I'd have to ask Ashley later what in the world was going on here, because I was completely baffled. "Yes, we flew."

Mr. Deaton just shook his head slowly. "They'll be wantin' to spot and tag bears again with those things, I'll wager," he mumbled. "They'll run us ragged lookin' for this one bear, now that it's happened twice."

"What's happened twice?" I asked quickly.

Mr. Deaton frowned. "Oh, this is the second

campsite this month that some bear's torn up. Those park rangers will go crazy now trying to find the bear, most likely. They'll fly all over creation and then want to relocate it. Like that does any good."

"What?" Ashley and I both asked at exactly the same time. We both laughed.

"It does no good to relocate a bear, is all," Mr. Deaton sighed. "Once a bear's gotten used to a park, he won't be any good anywhere else. You might as well go ahead and destroy him. Either that, or give him to a zoo, if there's one that'll take him."

"What if it's a grizzly?" I asked.

Mr. Deaton looked at me like I was a total moron. "No grizzlies around here anymore, son. None. They got rid of 'em years ago."

"Not even way out in the wilderness?" I persisted.

"I don't know where you heard such a fool story," Mr. Deaton said, his eyes blazing. "But talk like that scares people. I'm tellin' you. There aren't *any* grizzlies around here, and there aren't any grizzlies ripping up campsites. Period. If it was anything, it was a black bear with a cub, most likely."

"It was just a question," I almost whispered.

"Well, don't ask questions like that around here," Mr. Deaton said gruffly. "Now, I gotta go. We got a big meeting." He turned, but then turned back. "Say, you're new around here, aren't you?"

I nodded. "We just moved in, up the road."

"The cabin house?"

"Yeah. My stepdad's a—"

Ashley leaned into me and then knocked me over.

She did it deliberately. We both fell to the ground. She pinned one of my arms to the ground before I could roll free.

"Sorry," she mumbled. She rolled over onto her stomach and waved to her dad with a free hand. "See ya later, Dad. Can you maybe take us out to Needlepoint when you get back?"

"If there's time after we're finished chasin' bears," Mr. Deaton answered. He looked over at me. "Welcome to Ganymede, son. Don't let Ashley push you around too much." Then he turned and strode away to the back of the house. We heard the roar of a car engine a moment later. A Jeep whipped around the house and raced off in a cloud of dust.

"Man, he's in a hurry," I said.

"Always is when stuff like this is goin' on," Ashley said.

Mrs. Deaton looked down at the two of us on the ground. "I have chocolate chip cookies. Fresh baked. Are you interested, Josh?"

"Yeah!" I said, jumping up. This time, I beat Ashley to the front door. But not by much.

△

CHAPTER 12

△ I figured there would be this huge, monster headline in the local paper, something like KILLER BEAR ON THE LOOSE! That's the way it would be in Washington, D.C. Anytime something weird happens, the whole place goes slightly bonkers.

Like the time some lunatic took his high-powered rifle and camped out on a bridge that led into the CIA complex in Langley, Virginia, and picked off people in their cars as they drove into the place.

They shut down the road that went by the complex. They had about a zillion reporters all over the place, and you heard about it everywhere for two days. They made the lunatic famous instantly.

So I figured I'd see the same thing here. I mean, you had a bear on the loose out in the wilderness, ripping up campsites. It *had* to be big news.

But it wasn't. I mean, they didn't even have a newspaper that came to your house every day. Oh, you could get the *Los Angeles Times* delivered to you if you wanted. But that newspaper didn't give a hoot about what happened in the High Sierras, unless it was something like an avalanche or a major catastrophe.

There wasn't a big local TV news truck that zoomed around with fluffy-haired reporters sticking big cameras in people's faces, asking them goofy questions. There weren't any TV stations, unless you counted the dinky public TV station down the valley that liked to run 1927 movies and flower-and-garden shows.

No, word of the bear attacks definitely traveled a different route in the High Sierras. It traveled the old-fashioned way, from one person to the next.

We moved right into the cabin house. Mark figured, why not? The furniture was in storage, and he just asked the moving company to move it on out.

In fact, it was there when I got back from Needlepoint with Ashley. There were boxes in every room. My junk was up in the loft. Mom had even unpacked some of my stuff and laid it out on the floor. We were practically moved in.

Mark had been called away to a meeting, too, just like Mr. Deaton had been. It seemed like there were meetings all over the place. I wondered what they talked about at those meetings. Did they have big maps where they talked about all the possible places to look for the renegade bear?

When I asked Mr. Deaton about it on the way to Needlepoint, he didn't say much. Something about how they'd narrowed it down to three bears they'd tagged before, and how they'd be following their movements to see if one of them was the culprit.

"How do you follow a bear?" I asked.

"Very carefully," Mr. Deaton said with a perfectly straight face.

Ashley jumped right in. "What time is it when a big black bear sits on a park bench?" she asked. I didn't know. "Time to fix the bench," she guffawed. She was the only one laughing. Mr. Deaton didn't even crack a smile.

Mr. Deaton had swung by the cabin house and asked Mom if it was all right to take me to Needle-point. They'd talked briefly, while I held my breath. I wasn't exactly sure what Mom would say. Would she let me go off with some strange guy to a place she'd never seen or even heard of?

Sure, no problem, knock yourself out, she'd told me. Have fun. Be careful. Don't jump off any moun-taintops.

What was going on here? I'd wondered. Was there something in the mountain air that made Mom less worried about what I was doing?

In Washington, she'd watched my every move. She'd still watched me get on the school bus, like I was a baby or something. I had the feeling that she'd let me wander to school on my own out here.

Needlepoint was an amazing place. It was a rock face, but it was different than others I'd seen. It was honeycombed with openings you could crawl through on the way up to the top. Ashley said it was because water had once run down the side, making the openings.

At the top, the rock face actually came to a sharp point in one place. I started laughing. *"That's* why they called it Needlepoint," I said out loud.

"Yeah, and because there are all these holes the needle can weave in and out of, like we are," Ashley answered.

We wandered in and around the honeycombed rocks for a couple of hours or so, and then just sort of hung out on top of the rock face until Mr. Deaton came back to pick us up. It was great.

Ashley and I talked about the new junior high we'd both be going to at the end of summer vacation, what it was like around Jupiter. Ashley said she'd teach me how to ride and maybe we'd take a pack train together along the Muir Trail sometime.

"A pack train, like in the Old West?" I asked. "With mules and everything?"

"Sure, just like that."

The sun began to set while we were up on Needlepoint. We watched the shadows stretch out over the valley to the east of us. The valley seemed to catch fire. Parts of it turned orange in the fading sunlight.

"Orange trees?" I wondered aloud.

"It's a trick," Ashley said. "It always looks like that from a distance when the sun goes down."

While we were sitting there, just sort of staring up at the sky, two birds came screaming by. They were huge. They circled in and around each other as they winged through the sky.

"Eagles?" I asked.

"Nope, just hawks, out hunting for the evening," Ashley said matter-of-factly.

"But there *are* eagles around?"

"Sure. Way, way up in the High Sierra mountain ranges. Not down where we are. You really have to travel to get to where the eagles are. At least, where the few remaining eagles are in these parts."

We watched the hawks hunt for a while. It was interesting. They circled and played up in the sky, until finally one of them spotted a rabbit or something on the ground and then sort of fell out of the sky. The other went screaming after it.

When Mr. Deaton came back to get us, Ashley raced me down to the bottom. She killed me. I was only two thirds of the way to the bottom, stuck in one of the honeycombs when I heard her warlike victory yell. I would have to learn. No question about it.

By the time Mr. Deaton dropped me off at our new home, I was worn out from the day—finding our new house, meeting Ashley, trying to figure the whole place out, climbing Needlepoint. When my head hit the pillow in my new bunkbed, I was out in a flash.

△
CHAPTER 13

△I woke in a cold sweat. There had been something. I couldn't quite put my finger on it. Something had been there, something huge, looming before me, about to devour me.

Then I heard the *scratch, scratch* just out back of the house. I lay very still in my bunk and listened. There was definitely something out behind the house.

It was the strangest sound. I couldn't figure it. The noise wasn't like a dog that wants out of the house and scratches at the door to be let out. It had a different sound, not like claws on wood. Something else.

Finally, plucking up my courage, I slipped out of my bed and crept down the ladder silently, stealthily. Mom and Mark were sleeping peacefully in the master bedroom. I was careful not to make a sound.

The sounds were definitely coming from out back of the house, just off the stone porch that wrapped around on the second level.

I moved through the darkened house. I stayed back against the wall to the inside. I was careful not to let a moon shadow fall across the windows.

I vaguely remembered that there was one bank of windows that looked out over the back porch. I glided over to those and slowly eased up to a position where I could look out of a corner of the window.

The moon was nearly full, and there were no clouds in the sky, so I could see the porch clearly. I got up on one knee and stared out the window, looking for some clue to the sounds I'd heard.

There was a slight movement, out toward the corner of the house! I stared at the spot, not blinking. There it was again!

As my eyes adjusted to the dimness of the moonlight, I was able to make out the shape of a big plastic garbage can Mom had placed just outside the kitchen door, on the back porch.

That was what it was, the sound I hadn't been able to place. Claws against plastic! Of course. But what was the animal? I watched for several minutes before I could make it out.

It was a raccoon. I was surprised at how big it was. When it climbed up on its hind paws, it could actually reach the lid of the big garbage can.

The raccoon was very patient about it. It certainly seemed to be in no hurry. It stood there on its hind paws, jabbing at the lid over and over with its front paws, trying to push it off.

When I'd taken the garbage out that evening, I'd forgotten to put the metal fastener on the lid. I could tell because, whenever the raccoon was able to push the lid up a little, the fastener would clink and rattle.

It took the raccoon about five minutes or so to push the lid a few inches off to one side. And then, much to my surprise, the raccoon took one paw, grabbed the lid, and actually pulled it to the ground.

The raccoon jumped a little when the lid banged to the ground. It skittered off the porch and disappeared into the woods close by. But it was back in a minute or so, when no one came out to inspect the sound.

I kept deathly still. I didn't want to spook the raccoon. I'd never seen anything quite like this. I guess they had raccoons in Washington, D.C., but I sure had no idea how you actually saw one doing its thing like this.

The raccoon clearly had a problem now. The garbage can was taller than it. It had two choices if it wanted to get at some of the garbage inside—it could either try to climb inside, or it could pull the can over and spill the contents.

It chose the second option, apparently by design. I was starting to get the idea that it had done this kind of thing before. The raccoon sure seemed like an expert at it.

Instead of just hooking its small paws on the edge of the can and climbing over, the raccoon stood up on its hind legs, grabbed the edge with one paw, and began to rock back and forth. The can swayed back and forth and, finally, fell with a very loud *thud!*

91

The raccoon skittered away into the woods again, this time for three or four minutes. But when nothing moved in the house, it came back and began to inspect its booty with obvious relish.

It didn't just dig right in and begin ripping up bags. No, it pulled things out *very* slowly and just sort of nosed around in the garbage, smelling everything. It was quite choosy. And it was taking its time. But why not? It had all night to feast.

Finally, the raccoon seemed to settle on something, because it sat down on its haunches and began to work at opening a very small hole in one of the bags. I couldn't see what it was from my vantage point, but I had to think it was the plastic garbage liner Mom threw leftovers into.

The raccoon found something, took it in both of its paws and sat back to eat. It held the leftover—whatever it was—in both of its paws and nibbled at it very delicately. It did this for a long time.

When it was finished, it rocked forward slowly and nosed through the trash until it had found something else to its liking. It pulled it from the garbage bag slowly, cautiously, and then went through the same routine.

It reminded me of a finicky eater at a restaurant, carefully selecting his order from the menu and then savoring every bite. It didn't look like the campsite the bear had ransacked, that was for sure.

After the raccoon had gone through several courses of its gourmet meal, my knees were getting sore and my back was starting to hurt from hunching over, so I decided it was time to do something.

"Oh, Mr. Raccoon," I whispered.

The raccoon stopped eating. It looked up, and I could almost see its ears perk up and its whiskers twitch. It held the food out in front of its face, waiting for another sound.

I knocked on the window once. The raccoon didn't run right away. Its head moved slightly in my direction, but it remained where it was.

I crept over to the doors that led out to the back porch, keeping one eye on the raccoon. When I got to the door, I turned the handle as slowly as I could. It didn't squeak. Then I eased it open slowly.

The raccoon didn't run until it actually saw me come through the door. But, boy, did it bolt then! In fact, it skidded out on the porch because it tried to get away so fast. I'd clearly scared the daylights out of it.

I reached back inside the door and flipped on the light switch. The light was bright, and I had to squint for a moment. Then I walked over to the garbage can and inspected the damage.

The raccoon had pulled out most of the contents of the bag Mom kept in the kitchen. Nearly all the leftover food was pulled out and separated into little piles.

As I inspected the meal, I was quite surprised to see just how picky and choosy the raccoon had been. It hadn't touched anything with tons of grease or fat in it. French fries were still there. So was a piece of greasy hamburger. But the bun was gone, and the corn on the cob was picked clean.

"Totally weird," I said out loud.

I went back in the house, pulled out a new garbage bag, went back to the sight of the nighttime feast, and put the leftovers back in the new bag. When I put the bag back in the garbage can, I fastened the metal holders that kept the lid in place. I try not to make mistakes twice, if I can help it.

As I returned to the house and climbed the ladder to my loft, a warm, tingly sensation swept over me. I couldn't explain it. I just felt like I'd seen something special, like I'd gotten a chance to play God for a brief moment and peek into something I wouldn't ordinarily see.

It was cool. I liked it. I didn't blame the raccoon for ransacking our garbage. Far from it. If I was dumb enough to leave the garbage lid off, and the raccoon was smart enough to figure a way into it, well, then that was just fine with me. It seemed almost *natural.*

But I did wonder a little about how it was different for animals like raccoons that lived near humans. It changed their pattern of behavior. Perhaps a lot.

Just like bears that get used to feeding on garbage at parks, I thought dreamily as I drifted off to sleep again.

△
CHAPTER 14

△"Mom, where are the encyclopedias?" I asked at breakfast the next morning.

"Packed," Mom said groggily as she cradled a cup of coffee in her hands, sipping it slowly.

"In a place I can find them?"

Mom opened one eye and gave me a strange look. "Any particular reason?"

"I wanted to look something up."

"Because?"

"Because I wanted to, that's all."

"And you have to do it right now?"

"Well . . . yeah. I'd like to."

I really did want to figure out why they called our mountain Ganymede before I saw Ashley again that morning. But I felt kind of stupid telling Mom this, for some reason. I wanted to look it up myself first.

Mom grunted finally and got up from the kitchen table. I followed her through the front foyer and down the stairs to the huge stone cellar built into the mountain and down below. It was quite cool and dry below.

Mom pulled the light switch on and pointed off toward the far corner of the room. "There. Over in the corner. One of those boxes. But *do not* make a mess. If you do, I'll skin you alive."

"Don't worry, Mom. I won't."

I meandered over to the boxes and began to look through them. Mom had labeled them carefully, and it wasn't hard to find the box with the encyclopedias in it.

When I finally found the section for Ganymede, I laughed out loud. It was funny. These people around here apparently had a sense of humor.

Ganymede was one of the satellite moons of the planet Jupiter. It was the fourth moon, to be exact, and it was one of the largest planetary satellites in our solar system.

I also noticed that there was another Ganymede as well. In Greek mythology, apparently, there was a handsome Trojan boy named Ganymede whom Zeus carried off one day to wait hand and foot on the gods. Not exactly a great job, I thought ruefully.

So which Ganymede was this, I wondered? The satellite of Jupiter, or the cupbearer to the gods? Or were they, somehow, intertwined?

"So which bear do they think it is?" I asked Mark at the breakfast table.

"Not sure," Mark answered. "But I think we're gettin' closer."

It was just the two of us at the table. Mom was upstairs, probably trying to pry her eyelids open. Mark had been out the night before, until close to midnight. They'd been reviewing all the records they had on tagged bears, trying to come up with some idea about which one might be responsible.

"So you think you have it, like, narrowed down to an actual bear or something?" I asked.

Mark shook his head. "You know, I wish it were that easy. But it's not. . . ."

"How come?"

"Well, for one thing, the Sierra Nevadas are huge. I mean, the range covers a lot of territory. And there are so many bears."

"But didn't you say it was maybe one of the park bears?"

Mark looked up. "Who told you that?"

I was embarrassed, for some reason. "I, um, I thought it was you. Maybe it was Mr. Deaton."

"Ashley's dad?"

"Yeah, him, I guess. He's a forest ranger."

Mark nodded his head slowly, thoughtfully. "Hm, I see. That explains it."

"Explains what?"

Mark sighed. "Oh, it's all so silly. Like kids fighting over a spoon in a sandbox."

"What?"

"Well, let me put it this way: you have two services, and two types of rangers out here in a place like the High Sierras. You have people like me, the National Park Service rangers, who look after the

97

parks that get a lot of tourist traffic. And then you have the National Forest Service rangers, who look after the wilderness, essentially. We both serve different government agencies, and we both have different missions."

"And you both are looking for this bear?"

"That's right." Mark nodded. "We're both looking for this bear as fast as we can, before someone gets killed."

"So what's the big deal?"

"The big deal is that we have different ideas for going about it, and where the bear might be. The Forest Service guys, like Ashley's dad, blame the Park Service for letting bears get too close to humans and then relocating problem bears to other parts of the Sierra Nevadas by helicopter."

"And you probably think the Forest Service is messin' up, too?"

"Oh, I suppose. The Park Service tries to keep tight control over things. I mean, millions of visitors come through the parks, and we have to make sure trouble doesn't happen. The Forest Service looks after the wilderness, and they see things a little differently."

I wasn't entirely sure I understood what was going on here. But I could see it was bothering Mark. A lot. "So where's the bear?"

Mark reached over to a backpack slung across one of the kitchen chairs. He pulled a map from the back pouch, opened it, and spread it out on the kitchen table. I scooted my chair back and peered over his shoulder. "See the region?" he asked.

"Where are we?"

Mark pointed to Jupiter, and then moved his finger slightly east and traced the outline of the High Sierra National Park. Then he showed me where Redstone Canyon was in relation to both High Sierra and Yosemite National Park.

"Get the picture?"

I nodded. "Yeah, but isn't that a long way, from one place to the next?"

"Exactly. And that's the problem here. Redstone is a very long way from Yosemite or High Sierra. We've never relocated a problem bear anywhere close to Redstone, and there's just no way a black bear and a cub, or even a black bear traveling alone, is likely to go from a park to Redstone."

I shook my head. I was confused. "I don't get it. You mean, you don't think there's a bear, like you said, that got used to eating garbage and junk in one of the parks and then went after that campsite I saw?"

"Actually, yes, that's what I'm saying. But the Forest Service sees it otherwise. They think it's a park bear that went after that campsite."

"Why?"

"Because there was another incident, not too long ago, at a site just south of Yosemite. Someone's backpack and campsite were ripped apart at an overnight, and they figured it was a bear. Now, we have this incident at Redstone, and they feel sure it's the same bear, traveling south."

"But you're not so sure, are you?" I asked softly.

"Not at all. My gut tells me it's not the same bear. For one thing, Redstone's thirty miles or so south of the Yosemite incident. Plus, we've never heard of

99

bears around Redstone, though that wouldn't be too surprising because Redstone is fairly uncharted territory to begin with."

A thought occurred to me. "What about a grizzly? Have you asked around about that?"

"Yep, a little." He nodded. "There aren't any more grizzlies around here. That's the word."

"Not even one or two, like the stories say?"

"Nope. Not even one. A grizzly hasn't been seen in years. Last one was maybe a decade ago, up near the summit of Mount Solon."

"Where's that?"

Mark pointed to a mountain on the map. "Here."

"But that's real close to Redstone, isn't it?"

"I suppose. Redstone Canyon is down the mountain slope and off to one side. But that doesn't mean anything, Josh. Really. Trust me. The grizzlies are gone from here."

"OK," I said, not entirely convinced. "So what are you guys gonna do now, about finding the bear?"

"Well, we have it narrowed down to three likely suspects, all of them problem bears we relocated from Yosemite last summer," Mark said. "All three are out there in the wilderness, between High Sierra and Yosemite."

I could see that something was still eating at Mark. "But you really *aren't* sure, are you?"

Mark shook his head. "No, I'm not. But what do I know? I've been here less than a month."

"I dunno. You never know. So why do you think it isn't one of those three bears?"

"Because where we relocated those three bears isn't anywhere close to Redstone," Mark said. "In order to get there, all three would have needed to travel quite a distance, and I just don't think they would. It doesn't fit."

"So how will you track them?"

"With teams, in shifts, if we have to."

"Teams. And you'll be on one of them?"

"Yes, which means I could be gone for a number of days."

"Really?"

"We're going out with gear, and we'll track the bears both from the ground and the sky. But we can't use helicopters too much, because it'll spook the bears."

"So you're gonna, like, camp out and watch the bears?"

"Exactly."

"Wow. That's neat. I couldn't . . . um, you know, maybe come with you guys on this, could I?"

Mark smiled. "Sorry, kid. You got away with that once. But not this time. Mr. Wilson would skin me alive if I pulled a stunt like that. But I promise we'll go camping right when I get back."

"Promise?"

"Promise. It's a deal."

△
CHAPTER 15

△ Ashley and I left for Ju-
piter on our bikes after breakfast that morning. Ashley knew a back way, through the woods. Of course.
Ashley seemed to know where *everything* was.

It was hard to keep up. I could pedal faster than
her but, man, she was like a lunatic kamikaze dare-
devil biker. She jumped every big stick or stone she
came across and she skidded out around every turn.
No wonder she had about a billion cuts and bruises
on her arms and legs.

She ditched her bike near a stream deep in the
woods between Ganymede and Jupiter. I ditched
mine, too, and hurried to catch her before she disappeared.

"Wait up!" I called out finally in exasperation.

"Hurry!" she yelled back.

"Why?"

" 'Cause."

I gritted my teeth and sprinted after her. A branch whipped my face. It stung, but I ignored it.

"What's the hurry?" I asked breathlessly when I caught her.

Ashley slowed immediately and started to walk. "No hurry," she grinned.

I was about ready to brain her, but I kept my mouth shut. I'd get even somehow. "So what's the deal? Where are we goin'?"

"You'll see," she said mysteriously.

We walked for about five minutes. I could just barely make out the path Ashley was following. It wasn't really a path, like you'd find in some park. It was different. The grass was flattened out, and it was narrow.

"You know where you're goin', right?" I said after a while.

"Yep, I do."

"What is this?"

"The path?"

"Yeah, that."

Ashley smiled mischievously. "You mean you can't tell?"

"No, I can't," I said angrily. "So are you gonna tell, or do I just have to guess?"

"It's a deer path, silly. You can tell because of the flat grass, the way it's so narrow and because of the small, little . . . um, you know, things along the path."

I looked down at my feet. After a few steps, I spotted the little black droppings she was referring to. "Oh," I said lamely.

We came to a second stream. At least I thought it was a second stream, because it was a lot wider than the one where we'd ditched our bikes. Ashley just plowed right through, soaking the bottom of her pants. I picked out a few rocks and jumped from one to the next without getting my own pants wet.

"Hey, by the way, why're we walkin'? Why didn't we take our bikes?"

"Ssshhh!" Ashley whispered fiercely, dropping to her knees suddenly.

"What?" I hissed.

Ashley pointed. "See," she said softly.

I looked in the direction she was pointing, but gradually my eyes adjusted to the distance. I saw it, a small brown deer standing motionless between two trees. I could see its ears twitching nervously, back and forth. I started to get up. I wanted to move closer for a better view.

"Sit still," Ashley commanded. "You'll run it off."

"No, I won't," I said, feeling quite sure that I could move closer. "It's not going to—"

The deer bolted. It took two leaps and then darted away. It was gone in an instant. I felt like a total moron. How could I have been so dumb?

Ashley whirled on me, her eyes flashing. "Didn't I tell you not to—"

"Yeah, so?" I cut her off. "There's always more deer to see."

"And how many have *you* seen out in the woods, huh?"

"Enough," I huffed.

"Yeah, I'll bet," Ashley said, shaking her head.

"Well, let's keep going." She got up and kept walking, very briskly.

"You mind telling me where we're going, and why we didn't take our bikes?"

"She doesn't like contraptions like bikes, that's why."

"Who doesn't?"

"You'll see. And she doesn't like visitors, either, so keep your mouth shut until I tell you it's OK."

"What do ya mean, she doesn't like visitors? Who are you talking about?"

"Like I said, you'll see. She likes me, so just follow what I do. OK? We're almost there."

I was totally confused. Ashley was starting to drive me crazy, and I was beginning to wonder if she didn't have a couple of loose bolts banging around inside her skull.

But I also trusted her for some reason. She seemed so absolutely, totally sure of what she was doing. There seemed to be very little she couldn't do. Or wouldn't try, for that matter.

She suddenly dropped to one knee again and pointed. "See it?" she whispered.

"What?" I asked, squinting.

"There!" she said impatiently.

I tried to peer through the foliage, toward what looked like a small opening. There was something there, some sort of a structure. I stared for a long time until I could finally make out what it was.

"It's a shack," I said, turning to Ashley.

"Took you long enough."

"Yeah, well, we're pretty far away. So who lives there, anyway?"

"Bear Walks at Night."

I gave Ashley a funny look. "What?"

"Don't ask me. I call her Miss Lily."

"How come?"

"You'll see," Ashley said mysteriously.

"But her real name?"

"It's an Indian name," Ashley said. "I can't pronounce it. She's a Yokuts, and she actually has a Yokuts name. But that's what it stands for."

"Bear Walks at Night?"

"You got it."

"So what's it mean?"

Ashley got up and started walking toward the shack. "Let's go ask."

"Hey! Wait up," I called out. I got up quickly and hurried to Ashley's side. "So what's the deal? How come she lives way out here in the middle of nowhere?"

"She claims this is her land," Ashley said. "But don't ask her about it. Dad says the government took this land a long, long time ago. But she still claims it belongs to her people, so she stays here on it."

"And no one's ever kicked her off?"

Ashley shook her head. "Nope. Nobody has the heart. She lives out here all alone, tending her little garden for food, gathering wood for her fire."

We walked a little ways farther and then emerged into a meadow. I now saw why Ashley called her Miss Lily. There were white lilies, hundreds of them, all around the meadow. Lilies as far as the eye could see.

"Miss Lily," I snorted. Ashley only smiled.

The meadow was small, maybe several hundred yards wide. It was surrounded by tall trees on nearly all sides. A small creek meandered through the western side of the meadow.

The shack was tiny, maybe the size of one large room in a normal house. There was a thin stream of smoke curling out of what looked like a crude stone chimney.

An old, old woman was sitting in front of the shack. Her head was bent over something. I looked closer. It was a wide, flat rock. The old woman was slowly rubbing another rock over the bigger one.

"What's she doing?" I whispered close to Ashley.

"She's grinding corn," Ashley whispered back. "She grows it herself. Don't ask me how. She lets the kernels dry out, then she grinds it up like that into meal and bakes it. It's cool. Her bread is great."

"You've eaten here?"

"Sure. I come here a lot."

I didn't say anything as we approached. I remembered to let Ashley introduce me, and to keep my mouth shut. Which was just fine by me. For some reason, I was slightly terrified of this old woman living out here, alone, in a meadow full of lilies.

The old woman didn't look up until we were just a few feet from her. When she did, she looked first at Ashley, and then at me. Her old eyes, covered by folds of wrinkles, stared at me for the longest time. They seemed almost to burrow into me. It was all I could do to return the gaze.

"Your friend," she said to Ashley, "he is afraid. Tell him, please, not to be. Not of me. He has nothing to fear from me."

Ashley turned to me. "She says not to be afraid."

"I heard—" I started to answer. Ashley held her hand up so quickly, I stopped in midsentence.

"She *also* says," Ashley said, her eyes burning into mine, "that you have nothing to fear from her."

"OK," I said to Ashley, not to the old woman.

Ashley turned back to the old woman. "Can I help, with the meal?"

The old woman reached down and picked up a second smooth stone and handed it to Ashley. Ashley took the stone and knelt beside the large, flat rock. The old woman reached into a burlap sack, pulled a handful of dry corn kernels from it, and handed them to Ashley.

Ashley laid the kernels on the flat rock. She rolled her own stone gently over them, applying pressure, until I heard them begin to pop and crunch. Only then did she begin to press harder, grinding the kernels into fine meal.

"Miss Lily, my friend's name is Joshua," Ashley said after a little while. "He has just moved here, and he lives near me."

"He is your age?" she asked Ashley.

"Yes, he is."

"And does he always let the women do the work?" she asked Ashley.

"Not always," Ashley laughed. "Can he help, too, with the meal?"

"If he likes," the old woman answered. "Would he?"

Ashley looked over one shoulder. "Wanna help?"

I shrugged. "Sure."

The old woman handed a third rock to Ashley,

not to me, and then took kernels from her bag and laid them on the stone in front of Ashley. Ashley took them and handed both the rock and the kernels to me.

I knelt down beside Ashley, across from the old woman, and tried to follow the same routine Ashley had gone through. I rolled the kernels slowly. But nothing happened. I could see that both Ashley and the old woman were watching me like a hawk.

I applied more pressure. Still nothing. I gave one, big push hoping to crunch at least a couple of the dumb things. A kernel squirted out the side. Ashley giggled. A very small smile creased one corner of the old woman's mouth.

"He has not done this before, has he?" the old woman asked Ashley.

"He has not," Ashley said somberly, trying not to laugh again.

I reached out and snatched the kernel from the ground angrily. I was just about to put it back under my own rock, when the old woman held up a hand.

"Tell him to give it to me," she commanded of Ashley. "I will put it in my grow sack."

I reached out and placed the kernel in the old woman's gnarled, weather-beaten hand. Her hand was tough and leathery to the touch as I dropped the kernel in it. The old woman smiled at me for the first time as our hands touched. She took it and placed it in a second sack.

"What's that sack for?" I asked Ashley, not the old woman.

"It's her grow sack," Ashley said. "She takes kernels that aren't so hot, the ones that are sort of ugly

110

or gnarly, and then she plants them again. She doesn't grind them up for meal. Nothing's wasted, that way."

I nodded. "I see."

We stayed there for a long time, grinding meal. I finally got the hang of it. I figured out that you had to push straight down on the rock to crunch the stupid little kernels. If you didn't apply pressure evenly, it didn't work.

But once I got going, I ground up more meal than either of them. I was proud of it. I'd made a little pile of dusty, yellow meal by the time I was finished. Of course, I had absolutely no idea what to do with the stuff then. But I figured that wasn't my job anyway.

"That is enough for today," Miss Lily said. She knelt forward and lifted herself off the ground. It was hard for her. She was quite old, and her back almost seemed to creak and sway just from the effort of getting up.

"Will you cook?" Ashley asked.

"Not today," Miss Lily said, shaking her head. "But I would like a fire, for tea, perhaps."

Both Miss Lily and Ashley looked at me. *What!* I thought, somewhat wildly. *You're kidding, right! I'm supposed to figure out how to make a fire! So when did I become an Eagle Scout anyway!*

"Well?" Ashley asked impatiently.

"Deep subject . . ." I grimaced.

"Ha, ha, very funny," Ashley said. "So are you gonna get the firewood or not?"

I sighed. "Sure. No problem." I looked around, hoping maybe that the old woman had a little pile already gathered and that I could maybe just walk over and gather a handful. No such luck. The dirt was swept clean around her little shack and there wasn't a scrap of wood anywhere close by.

So I traipsed back to the woods silently and started scrounging for wood. I had no idea what I was looking for, of course, so I gathered everything I could find—big sticks, little sticks, long and short, stubby and skinny, plus a handful of small twigs. I stumbled back to the hut with my arms full of wood, sticks and twigs trickling out both sides.

Ashley about fell over. "You plannin' to start a fire for an army or somethin'?"

"You wanna do this yourself?" I growled.

"OK, I will," she said, and promptly ran to the woods. She was back a minute later with one big log, several sticks, and a handful of twigs. She knelt down before a hollow in the ground, while the old woman went inside the hut.

As Ashley quickly piled the sticks and twigs in pyramid fashion, the old woman returned carrying a metal rod with a hook and a kettle on it. She handed the kettle to me. I took it and continued to stare at Ashley.

Miss Lily handed the flint and steel to Ashley, who took them and struck them together. Sparks flew. After several tries, the shower of sparks caused some of the twigs to begin to glow orange. Ashley blew on the pile gently until a flame emerged. Then she fanned the flame until it had become a fire. She piled more sticks and twigs on it, and finally placed the small log on it.

"There," she said with satisfaction. She turned to me. "Well?"

112

"Well, what?" I asked irritably.

"Where's the water?"

I stared at her numbly and then glanced down at the kettle in my hand. "Oh." I ran over to the stream, filled the kettle, and ran back. Ashley took it from me and hung it on the hook that was now over the fire.

There were three kiln-fired cups on the flat rock. I glanced in them. There were crushed leaves of some sort in each cup. We sat there silently and waited for the water to boil. Then Ashley took the kettle down carefully and poured the water.

After a minute or so, Miss Lily and Ashley began to carefully pick out the crushed leaves. The water had turned a dark green. It smelled a little like peppermint.

It took forever to pick the dumb leaves out. There were about a thousand of the things. Every time I thought I'd found them all, another one would float to the surface.

"A coupla leaves won't kill ya," Ashley laughed.

I looked up. They were both sipping their tea while I obsessed over finding every last leaf. Chagrined, I put the cup to my mouth and took a sip.

"Ouch!" I yelled, as the scalding liquid about melted my tongue.

"It's hot," Ashley said mildly.

"I can *see* that."

"No, you can feel it."

I didn't say anything. I blew on the tea and tried another sip, a smaller one this time. I couldn't taste

113

a thing. My taste buds had already fled at the first sight of this concoction.

"Good, huh?" Ashley said.

I grunted noncommittally. I kept sipping until my mouth wasn't so numb from the shock.

"You are a stranger to the Earth?" Miss Lily asked me after a while.

I looked over at her. I couldn't believe it. She was actually speaking to me. "What?"

"You are a stranger to the Earth?" she repeated.

"You haven't been outside much," Ashley translated. "Camped, hiked, climbed rocks, junk like that."

"Oh, well, yeah, I guess so," I said. "I mean, I've camped a little. Before. Not so much lately."

"So you are a stranger." Miss Lily nodded. "And you seek wisdom?"

"I do?"

"Yes, you do," Ashley said quickly.

"I guess I do," I muttered.

Miss Lily looked at me again, those eyes boring into mine. "You have one question, I think. What is it?"

I returned her gaze this time. One question? What was she talking about? And then it came to me. Yes, I did have a question. But it seemed stupid.

"Why do they call you Bear Walks at Night?" I asked.

She smiled. Perhaps it wasn't such a stupid question after all. "Because I was born on a night when the Great Bear walked beside our homes."

"The Great Bear?"

"You call it the grizzly."

114

I hesitated. "There *are* grizzlies around here, then?"

"Once."

"But not now?"

"There is one, still. At least. Perhaps more."

"How do you know?"

The old woman looked off in the distance, toward the east. "When I was younger, when I could walk in the hills, I would see its signs everywhere. The Great Bear walked."

I looked over at Ashley. She shrugged. "But that was, um, a while ago?" I asked.

The old woman still looked off in the distance. "Yes, it has been a while. But the Great Bear walked. And this I know. It still walks today. My heart is sure."

"You said you saw its signs," I asked, curious. "What's that mean?"

"The Great Bear walks. It is afraid of nothing. It can take a buffalo down. Unlike the other bears, it does not climb a tree out of fear . . ."

"Grizzlies can't climb trees?"

"The Great Bear will *not* climb a tree. It has no need."

"And it could chase down a buffalo?"

"If it desired. Neither will it remain hidden in a cave, like the others, throughout the winter. It hunts, even in the coldest heart of the storms."

"Grizzlies don't hibernate?"

"It has no need."

"And there are signs?"

The old woman nodded. "We would burn the oaks, when I was a very young girl, so the berry

115

bushes would grow. And the Great Bear would come. It likes the berry bushes."

"Berry bushes?"

"Berry bushes." Miss Lily smiled. "It likes berries. But I would also see a deer taken down. Only the Great Bear does that."

"But hunters also shoot deer. Just because—"

"Hunters do not break their necks and eat the flesh of deer," the old woman said quietly.

"Oh," I said.

A funny thought occurred to me. "You've never actually *seen* the Great Bear?"

"No," the old woman said wistfully. "I have not. It is the one sadness of my life, that my eyes have not embraced the Great Bear."

"Eyes embraced?" I asked, perplexed.

The old woman looked back at me. "The Great Bear knows fear and courage, weakness and strength. If you show fear or weakness, it will devour you. But if you show courage and strength—if it sees that in your eyes—it will turn away. The legends say so."

"And how will it know?"

"It will know," the old woman said slowly, "as every other creature of the forest knows. It will look at you as the highest creature of God. If you act as something else, then you are doomed."

△
CHAPTER 16

△We stayed with Miss Lily most of the afternoon. She seemed to know so much about nature. I was astonished at her knowledge. It seemed endless. She knew story after story about nearly every animal that roamed the forest.

She told me about my raccoon, for instance. She told me what the raccoon would eat, and what it would not eat. She told me how to befriend that raccoon, which I vowed to try.

She also taught me how to bring the deer to my back door as well. A salt lick would do, she said. Especially in winter, when it was hard to find the grass.

But she didn't say much more about the Great Bear. Only that, once, she had seen many, many signs of it "walking" near a jagged peak that seemed to look like a ram's head. It seemed a little silly to me to compare a mountain to a ram's head, but I said nothing about it.

I was utterly fascinated with Miss Lily, and I could see why Ashley went there often. She lived so simply, perhaps as her people once had. There was very little she wanted or needed.

Nature was her friend, her constant companion, her shelter and her source of sustenance. There was almost nothing she needed that she could not find beside her in the forest.

She seemed so at peace with her world, with nature. She was no "stranger to the Earth," as I was. But, I finally concluded as I listened to her, she also did not *worship* the Earth, as so many foolish people who didn't know any better seemed to do these days.

I asked Miss Lily what she thought of God at one point. She had looked around her. You cannot see? she'd asked.

God is nature? I'd asked.

Some have made that mistake, she'd said, worshiping the creation and not the Creator. Her own people had made that mistake once.

But now, after so many years of observing, she'd said, it was very clear to her that God and creation were both magnificent, but distinct. Intertwined, but separate.

Again, I wasn't entirely sure I understood. I *thought* I did. It seemed awfully, awfully hard to tell the difference between the majesty of nature— which you could see—from the majesty of God, whom you could not see.

But you *can* see Him, Miss Lily had reasoned. You

can see His work everywhere. A reason, a time, a place for everything. Nothing by chance. It all worked together, she'd said.

Perhaps, I'd said at last. I would have to think about it.

Mark was planning to leave for his part of the expedition in the morning. They were taking a Land Rover out to Redstone and Mount Solon.

As it turned out, there was special urgency to the hunt now. The bear had struck again, during the night.

A troop of Eagle Scouts had been out camping, just a few miles off the Muir Trail near Mount Solon and Redstone. In the middle of the night, a bear had come into the camp and had ripped up the tent where two of the boys had been sleeping.

No one had seen a thing, really. By the time the camp had gotten up, the bear was long gone. But the tent had several long rake marks in it, and one side was pretty well tattered. It had been a bear. No question about it.

Mark's group was going to the north face of Mount Solon. A helicopter pilot claimed to have spotted a bear moving through the woods up the slope, so Mr. Wilson had reasoned that it was worth exploring, Mark said.

I had trouble sleeping that night. I kept counting bears instead of sheep. They jumped out at me from behind trees, leaped at me from dark caves, and rushed at me across small streams.

I was dead tired in the morning. I just barely managed to drag myself downstairs to see Mark off.

"Be careful," Mom said as they embraced.

"I will," Mark said. He turned to me. "You know, Josh, if you and Ashley want, you can listen in on the radio at the station. You can keep track of our progress. It might be fun."

I brightened a little. "Really? We can do that?"

"Sure, why not?" Mark said. "If your mom will drive you there."

I turned to Mom. "Would you?"

She smiled. "If you like."

"Yeah! That'd be great," I said. "I'll go tell Ashley." I turned to sprint out the door on Mark's heels.

"Whoa!" Mom said. "Breakfast first. You can call Ashley later."

"But . . ."

"Breakfast first. Sit," Mom commanded.

"Oh, Mom," I grumbled, making a face. But I obeyed. I sat down at the table and started to shovel food in my mouth.

"Slow down, Ace," Mom warned. "We can't leave right away anyway. It'll take a while for them to get there."

"Mom!" I groaned. "But Ashley . . . ?"

"Will still be there when you've finished. Relax. You don't have to take everything in one gulp."

Mom was right, of course. She usually was. Ashley hadn't even started her breakfast when I finally called. But she definitely wanted to go listen to the hunt for the marauding bear.

Mom talked to Mr. Wilson for a little while when we arrived. I couldn't tell if he was all that happy about the prospect of keeping track of Ashley and me for the day, but he didn't say anything. Mom told us she'd be back to get us sometime in the afternoon. OK, fine, I said, not paying a whole lot of attention.

The station was nearly deserted. Almost all of the rangers were out with one of the three teams, Mr. Wilson explained as we joined him in the "war room."

They'd changed the main cabin of the station. There were big maps of the various areas tacked up on the walls, plus charts of the three teams and notes beside each explaining their progress so far.

I walked over to one of the charts and looked at Mark's team. There were just notes explaining that they'd left in the morning and where they intended to explore.

I walked back over to the big round table in the center of the room, where Mr. Wilson had placed the big ham radio that he operated to keep in touch with the three teams. I took a seat in one of the high-backed chairs at the table. Ashley was off on the other side of the room, looking at the other charts and maps.

"Mr. Wilson, what will you do when you find the bear?" I asked him.

Mr. Wilson looked up from the table, still deep in thought. He was mapping this thing out like a general immersed in a battle. I could see his thoughts were a long way off. "Oh, I suppose we'll have to destroy it," he said somewhat distantly.

"Destroy it? What if you're not sure it's the right bear?"

"We don't have much choice, do we? We have to be cautious," Mr. Wilson said.

"But what if it's just a regular old bear that's out mindin' its own business?" I persisted.

"Joshua," Mr. Wilson said impatiently. "My rangers know what they're doing. If they find that bear, they'll know if it's the right one. There will undoubtedly be some clue that it's the right one."

"Like what?"

Mr. Wilson glared at me. I got the distinct impression he didn't like playing Twenty Questions like this. "Why don't you and Ashley take a hike for about an hour or so, until the rangers get to the sites? Nothing much is going to happen for a while."

"Um, OK," I mumbled. I wandered over to where Ashley was standing and tugged on her sleeve.

"What?" she asked, annoyed.

"Mr. Wilson says nothin' much will happen for a while, and that maybe we should take a hike for a while."

"But I don't want to miss anything."

I glanced over at my shoulder. Mr. Wilson was still looking at charts. "I don't think we will."

"Oh, all right," Ashley sighed.

We walked out into the bright sunshine. I stopped for just a second and looked around. It still absolutely astounded me how much clearer things looked here.

It was almost as if God had added an extra portion of color to everything—the leaves on the trees were just a little greener, the sky a little bluer—and thrown in a little bleach to make the clouds seem whiter.

I know it sounds silly. But the air was always so crisp and clear. Every time I took a deep breath, I sort of felt like running around, jumping and hopping and skipping. Of course, I didn't do that. I wouldn't. I mean, that would look dumb.

We decided to follow a stream for a ways. It was one of the many things I remembered from my father. If you're ever lost in the woods, try to find a stream and follow it back to your source.

It's what the animals do, he'd said. They all use streams and rivers and lakes as guides. The Indians did it as well. That's why so many of the roads in the Old West followed along rivers. It made sense.

Today, of course, there wasn't any need to do that. We had a million concrete rivers everywhere, going off in all directions. There was no need to worry about following creeks or streams anymore. And if you got lost, you just dialed 911.

We were gone a long time, much longer than an hour, as it turned out. Ashley got really interested in one particular creekbed. She kept trying to find this stupid cricket.

It was maddening. We could both hear the sound it made as it rubbed its legs together. But just as we thought we'd tracked the source, we'd look under a log or a rock, and no cricket. What did the thing do, throw its voice like a ventriloquist?

Ashley finally found the thing at the bottom of a hollow tree stump. She was so mad by then that she just climbed inside the stump and jumped up and down until the cricket was flat as a pancake.

"I thought you liked animals," I teased.

"I do," she huffed when she was finished.

"But a cricket's an animal, too."

"I don't care. It was drivin' me nuts."

"But it's still an animal," I insisted. "God made crickets, too."

"Well, then He made a mistake," Ashley shot back, "because all they do is drive you crazy."

"Um, I don't think God makes mistakes."

"Hmm," she grunted, and started off in some other direction to get out of the conversation.

But I knew I was right. Crickets are animals, too. They *had* to serve some useful purpose, even if it was only as food for the frogs in the creekbed.

Of course, they sort of drove me nuts, too. But I didn't tell Ashley that.

When we got back to the ranger station, the sun was well up in the sky and it had started to get hot. It had to be after noon. We took our jackets off, slung them over a railing on the front porch of the main cabin, and went inside.

We both took a seat at the big table, opposite Mr. Wilson. He barely looked up as we came in. There was a heavy frown on his face, and he was deep in thought.

I glanced at Ashley. Something was wrong. I could tell. So could she. But we both kept quiet and just watched to see what was happening. Neither of us wanted to interrupt Mr. Wilson to ask him.

"Three to base, three to base!" an urgent voice crackled over the radio.

Mr. Wilson grabbed the microphone and mashed the Talk button hard. "Base!" he practically growled. "I read. Whatcha got?"

"No sign of them yet," said the voice. I was pretty sure it was Mike Jennings. I thought I recognized the voice.

124

"What do you mean?" Mr. Wilson barked. "How can there be no sign of them? Over."

"Um, well, we took two wide circles out, in both directions, and we can't find a sign or a clue," Mike said. "It's, um, well, it's like they've just *vanished*. Over."

Mr. Wilson's jaws were bulging he was so angry. "Look! I don't care what it takes, you find those two. And quick! You have about four hours before you lose the sun behind the mountains. Over."

"But, sir, *how* do we do that?" Mike pleaded. "We've sent up flares now. We've canvassed the entire area—"

Mr. Wilson slammed the microphone down. "*Find* them!" he roared. "I don't care what it takes. Just get it done! Over!"

"Yes, sir," Mike answered miserably. "I'll report back in twenty minutes. Over and out."

Mr. Wilson switched off the microphone. He just stared at it for a few moments, and then looked over at me. Not at Ashley. At me. That's when I knew.

"Mark's missing, isn't he?" I asked, my voice quivering. There was a huge lump in my throat, and it was all I could do to keep from bursting into tears.

"Yes, son, I'm afraid so," Mr. Wilson said, his voice as gentle now as it had been gruff and angry just a moment before. "He and Dickerson went off separately an hour ago, and we've lost contact with them."

"But that doesn't mean . . ."

"No, no, it doesn't mean a thing, necessarily," Mr. Wilson said quickly. "It just means we've lost contact. They could turn up any minute now.

They're pros. I'm sure there's nothing to worry about."

"But why'd he leave the others?" I said, fighting back the tears.

Mr. Wilson closed his eyes. "Because they thought they'd spotted something. You see, they'd just found another camp—"

"*What?*" Ashley and I both said at the same time.

"There was blood on the ground from where the bear had dragged someone," Mr. Wilson said evenly. "They think a little boy who was out there with his father."

Ashley started to cry. My eyes burned like crazy. "A little boy?"

"His father was unconscious, mauled by the bear. And the boy was gone, dragged into the woods."

A cold, cold chill made me shudder. "And Mark thought he saw something, and went after it?"

"He did," Mr. Wilson said. "Now we've lost radio contact. But Josh, don't worry, I'm sure he's fine. Dickerson's a real pro. He's been doing this for a long time. I'm sure everything's fine."

"I wanna go there," I said suddenly, knowing how absurd and foolish the request was. But I *had* to go. There was no choice, really. I had to be out there, where Mark was.

"That's not possible . . ."

"Mr. Wilson, you *have* to let me," I said through a throat dry as cotton. "You just have to."

Mr. Wilson looked at me for a brief moment, then he looked away. I wasn't sure what he was staring at. But he'd made his decision when his old, weather-beaten face turned toward me. "All right.

Get your mom's permission and we'll head on out there. I should probably take a look at the scene anyway. But we're coming right back. Got it?"

"Yes, sir," I said sharply.

"The phone's over in the office," he ordered. "Go give your mom a call."

"And Ashley?" I asked.

Mr. Wilson shook his head. "She'll have to stay here with one of the rangers until your mom can come pick her up this afternoon."

"But—" Ashley started to protest. But she stopped when she saw the look in Mr. Wilson's eyes. There was no arguing this one.

"Move!" Mr. Wilson barked. "We don't have much time."

I moved.

CHAPTER 17

△The phone rang forever. Mom wasn't there. She was probably just out shopping or something. But I had a choice now.

I was sure Mr. Wilson would want to know that Mom had said it was all right for me to go. I knew that. But I also knew that I just *had* to get out there. So what could I do? If I told him Mom wasn't there, he wouldn't let me go. I was sure of that.

So I decided to lie about it. I made up my mind on the way back to the big round table with all the maps. I said a silent "sorry" to God. I tried to justify it, make it square, somehow. But I couldn't. It was wrong. It was just that I really wanted to get out there. It was like I had no choice.

"Your mom said it was OK?" he asked.

"Um, yeah, she did," I lied, quickly averting my eyes.

"Is she coming right here, to wait and make sure Mark's all right?"

"Yeah, that's what she said," I said, getting myself in even deeper.

"She wasn't too worried, was she?"

"Um, well, yeah, she was kinda worried. But she knows Mark can take care of himself."

Mr. Wilson pursed his lips. "Yes, he can." He glanced around the place. "All right, then, let me gather up some gear and then we'll be off. Why don't you go wait out in the Jeep? It's parked right out front."

I felt terrible. But what choice did I have, really? If I waited for Mom to get back, Mr. Wilson would be long gone. I *had* to do it this way. Didn't I?

Ashley followed me out to the car. She was awfully quiet. "You know, I keep thinkin' about that little boy," she said finally.

"Yeah, me too," I mumbled.

"I mean, what if it was you, or me?"

"I know."

"It's horrible. I just keep seeing it in my mind—that bear draggin' the little boy off, to a cave somewhere, maybe, you know . . ."

"Yeah," I said quickly. I swallowed hard. "But maybe he's OK?"

"Yeah, maybe." Ashley stared at me then. It made me uncomfortable. It was like she could see right through me. "Your mom wasn't home, was she?"

I blinked once, twice, three times. My throat was still dry. "How?" I finally managed to croak.

Ashley smiled wanly. "You're a lousy liar. It's all

over your face. I can't believe Mr. Wilson bought it. I could see it right off."

"But why didn't you say anything?"

" 'Cause." Ashley shrugged. "I'd probably do the same thing if it was my dad out there."

"Even though it's wrong to lie?"

"Yeah, I guess. I dunno. Sometimes you do things you know are wrong. You just do 'em anyway, and get walloped afterward. Know what I mean?"

"Yeah, I know." I frowned. "But I wish I didn't have to. I'm gonna catch it later. I know I will."

"Yep, you will," Ashley laughed. "No question about it. I'll tell your mom you're real sorry. Maybe it'll help." Mr. Wilson emerged from the doorway then. Ashley gave me a high-five. "Good luck."

Mr. Wilson threw his pack into the back of the Jeep, climbed in without a word, started the Jeep, and roared off. I turned and waved at Ashley. She waved back.

Mr. Wilson drove like a wild man through the forest. He'd clearly done this kind of thing before. He seemed to know where every tree root was. We whipped along a dirt path that was just barely visible to me, but was clearly seen by him.

It took us about a half hour to get there, I figured. Mr. Wilson didn't say anything for the entire trip. He kept his eyes riveted on the path before us. Which was fine with me. I wasn't sure I felt like talking anyway.

Mr. Wilson used the radio in the Jeep to locate the camp once we were close. It was about a mile or so off the Muir Trail—the main hiking trail through the Sierra Nevadas in this part of the country. The

131

camp was pitched in a little clearing between a stand of trees.

There were five rangers there when we arrived. Mark wasn't one of them. He and Dickerson were still missing, and there had been no radio contact.

The boy's father had been flown by helicopter to the nearest hospital. He'd lost a lot of blood from a blow to the head.

"He kept muttering about *two* bears," one of the rangers reported to Mr. Wilson shortly after we'd arrived.

"Two bears?"

"That's what he said," the ranger said. "The way he told it, the first bear came at them from the top of that tree—"

"From the tree?"

The ranger turned and pointed to a small pine about fifty feet or so from where they stood, at the perimeter of the small clearing. "Yes, sir. He said the bear climbed down the tree and attacked them."

Mr. Wilson walked over to the pine tree. We all followed him. He inspected the ground around the tree, then glanced up it. There were clearly claw marks on the bark of the tree from where the bear had either ascended or descended the tree.

At the bottom of the tree, there were fierce claw marks, as if the bear had been trying to get at something in the tree. Nearly all of the bark had been stripped.

"This is one angry bear," Mr. Wilson muttered under his breath.

"Seems so," the other ranger agreed.

"So what's this about a second bear?" Mr. Wilson

demanded, shading his eyes against the sun that was just starting to dip into the tree line to the west.

The ranger shrugged. "He said the first bear came at him, took a swipe at him and almost knocked him unconscious. And then he said a second bear, bigger than the first, came in right after."

Mr. Wilson sighed. "You're sure?"

"That's what the man said." The ranger nodded. "Then he said he lost consciousness, until we arrived."

"And his boy?"

"He doesn't remember anything about that. Nothing."

"So it's possible the boy ran off?"

"Yes, I suppose it's possible, but . . ." The ranger glanced over in another direction.

"Show me," Mr. Wilson said.

We walked over to a spot about twenty feet or so from the tree where the bear had come at them. There was a brownish-red stain in the dirt and grass. It was clearly blood. From there, we followed a trail of blood until it disappeared into the brush.

"Like I said . . ." The ranger's voice faded as we all stared at the trail of blood that led off into the deep wilderness.

A terrible aching swallowed me up. I felt so very, very sorry for that little boy. I only hoped that he had died quickly, before he'd been too terrified of what was happening to him. I couldn't imagine any fate worse than the one we were all witnesses to.

And then, out of nowhere and everywhere at once, a distant note sounded. Small, but insistent, at first, it eventually grew in intensity until I could ignore it no longer.

It was a cry. I was *sure*. But why could no one else hear it? I looked around, panicked. All the rangers were just milling around the clearing, minding their own business. They couldn't hear it.

But I could. It was there, plain as day. It was a cry for help. It was like one long note from a trumpet that lifted up over and through the trees of the wilderness.

"Can't anyone hear that?" I finally asked, impatient.

"What's that, Josh?" Mr. Wilson asked, turning to face me.

"That . . . that cry, that sound," I stammered. "Can't anyone hear it?"

Mr. Wilson and the other ranger paused for a moment and listened. After a few seconds, they both looked back at me. "No, son, I can't," the ranger said.

"Me, neither, Josh," Mr. Wilson added. "Sorry."

"But . . . but it's there. A cry. A note. *Something.*"

Mr. Wilson shook his head. "I'm sorry, Josh, but we just don't hear it."

I turned away. The note grew more insistent in my mind. But I was so confused now. Was it something only I could hear?

I looked off in the distance, toward the mountain peak that rose through the trees off to our east, away from the setting sun. That was the direction it was coming from. I was certain of it now. But what did it mean? *What*, exactly, was I hearing?

And then I knew. I *knew*. I was certain of it.

"The little boy's alive!" I almost shouted. "He is! I know it—"

Mr. Wilson frowned. "Josh . . ."

"I'm sorry, son, but I just don't see how it's possible," the other ranger said. "With so much blood, it just doesn't seem possible. I mean, we'd all like to hope, but it just doesn't seem reasonable."

I looked directly at Mr. Wilson. "Please?" I pleaded. "Can we at least go look for him? Please? Can we try now, before it's too late?"

"But, Josh, we have no idea where to start," Mr. Wilson offered, trying to sound reasonable. "The bear could have gone anywhere."

I pointed toward the mountain. "Over there," I said. "That's where we look."

"Mount Solon?"

"There," I repeated. "I know it."

Mr. Wilson turned to the other ranger. "There's a logging trail up the slope, isn't there?"

The ranger nodded. "Yeah, sure, I think I remember one. But it's long overgrown. There hasn't been anyone up that way, I'll bet, in a decade. No one's been out this way much in a long time. It's pretty isolated out here."

"But I can get up near the top with a four-wheel?" Mr. Wilson insisted.

"Probably," the ranger said reluctantly.

Mr. Wilson turned back to me. "You don't want to wait here for Mark to return?"

That hit me like a thunderclap. Where was Mark? What had happened to him out here? How did he figure in all of this?

135

"I . . . um, I don't really know, I guess," I managed. "I mean, is there anything we can do here, except wait for him?"

"That's about the size of it," Mr. Wilson said.

I made my decision. "Well, then let's go look. Maybe Mark'll be here when we get back?"

"I've seen enough here. And I suppose I can monitor developments here by radio, listen to see if Mark returns," Mr. Wilson mused. "All right, Josh, you win. Let's roll. We'll see what's out there."

Great, I thought. *I'm not sure I want to know.*

△
CHAPTER 18

△ Mount Solon towered in front of us. It went up and up, until it disappeared into a ring of clouds at the summit. From a distance, it had been pale gray at the top from the snow, fading into purple and brown. But up close, it just seemed to rise straight up to the heavens.

I was surprised that Mr. Wilson hadn't asked me why I was so certain that there was something here. I was glad he didn't, because I wasn't sure I could answer him.

The note—or *whatever* it was—was now a memory. I could still hear its faint echo, but that was all. I wasn't even sure, in fact, that I'd even heard it. Perhaps I'd imagined it.

There was a logging trail, it turned out, that wound its way upward from the base of the mountain, along the north side. Or at least there had been a trail *once.* Years and years ago, perhaps. Now it was nothing more than a weed-choked opening through the trees littered with large boulders. It was clear no one had been here for a very long time.

But Mr. Wilson was pretty good at keeping to the track that had once been there years ago. He picked his way carefully through the big boulders that were strewn everywhere, and was able to wind his way around the small trees that had grown up in the path that had been there once.

"You should know," Mr. Wilson said gruffly, "that I'm doing this because this is the north face."

"The north face? What's that mean?"

"It's where my chopper pilot said he saw a bear moving."

I remembered. "Oh, yeah, that's right."

"So this is worth a look," he said, keeping his eyes on the task at hand.

"Yeah, sure, course," I said quickly.

We drove in silence for about fifteen minutes or so, I guessed. It was work getting up this trail. We were making real slow progress.

Even in the middle of all this, it was hard not to at least notice the wonder and majesty of what was all around me. As we climbed higher on the mountain slope, I could begin to see glimpses of the untamed Sierra Nevada wilderness spread out beneath us.

It went on and on for as far as the eye could see. No factories, no big super highways, no apartment complexes, nothing like that. Just an endless ocean of trees, broken occasionally by a stream or a lake.

I couldn't see Redstone Canyon from this side of the mountain, but I could make out several other canyons off in the distance. Each was like a small, contained house or something, with steep cliff walls rising on either side and a river running through the middle of each. It probably went on like that for miles, I figured.

The radio crackled. Mr. Wilson reached for it quickly. "Wilson here. Come in. Whatcha got?"

"Good news, sir," the voice said. "Our two wayward rangers have returned, safe and sound. Dickerson said their radio just conked. He doesn't know why."

Mr. Wilson leaned back in the seat and took a deep breath. He looked over at me. My eyes were blinking furiously to keep the tears of joy at bay.

"That's great," Mr. Wilson said gruffly. "They see anything while they were out on their little adventure?"

"Nothin'. Absolutely nothin'."

Mr. Wilson nodded once, to no one in particular. "All right. We'll be back shortly. You all plannin' to set up camp there for the night?"

"We are, right now," the ranger answered.

"See you there, then." Mr. Wilson flipped the switch on the radio to the Off position. "Bet you're glad to hear that Mark's safe, right?"

"Yes," I said, my head bowed. And I was. I liked Mark. He wasn't my dad, but I did like him a whole lot. And I knew Mom loved him. So I was glad. I really and truly was. I hadn't known how worried I was, I guess, until I'd heard that he was safe.

"You're sure about that?"

I glanced over at Mr. Wilson. "Yeah, I'm sure!" I snapped.

139

"Mark's a good man, you know. Your mom's lucky."

"I know," I said. I rubbed my chin violently. My head twitched. "Man, let's get goin', OK?"

"Sure." Mr. Wilson smiled. "Good idea."

The mountain started to get quite steep. The Jeep was probably working its way up a forty-five-degree angle by now, and the trail had all but disappeared. We were making our way through deep wilderness that man probably hadn't visited in a long, long time.

"When did they log here, d'you think?" I asked.

"Hard to say." Mr. Wilson didn't take his eyes off the road. "I wouldn't be surprised if it's been twenty years or so."

"Twenty years!"

Mr. Wilson nodded. "Sure. Judging by the size of the trees that have grown up in the middle of this trail, I'd say it's been at least that since anyone's been this way."

I leaned back in my Jeep seat. Twenty years was an eternity. How was it possible that there was *anywhere* that hadn't been trampled by tourists in twenty years?

As I was leaning back, I happened to look up through the trees. There was a huge bird of some sort circling up quite high. Then I saw another, and then several more. There was a whole crowd of the birds circling high. And even though they were quite distant from us, I could see that they were *huge.*

"Mr. Wilson, look!" I said, pointing at the birds. "What are they?"

140

Mr. Wilson took his foot off the gas long enough to glance up. A dark scowl crossed his face when he spotted the birds. "That's it, then," he muttered.

"What is? What are they?"

"California condors." Mr. Wilson's eyes were still riveted on the birds circling lazily overhead. "Vultures. They feast on carrion."

"Carrion?"

"A dead carcass of some creature," Mr. Wilson said slowly. "They'll wait while a cougar or a bear or even an eagle, perhaps, has made a large kill and then come in for the scraps afterward."

"Does that mean . . . ?" I left the question hanging.

"Perhaps," Mr. Wilson said. "Who knows? But they're waiting for *something,* that's for sure."

I shuddered. I tried not to think about what the condors were waiting for. I strained to get a better look at them, but they were still pretty far away. All I could make out was that they had a very large wingspan, and they seemed to have no feathers on their neck, which seemed to jut out.

Mr. Wilson settled back in his seat. A look of hopeless despair swept across his face. "There's nothing more we can do here, Josh. It'll take a methodical search, and we can't really get all the troops out here until tomorrow, at first sunlight."

"But it'll be too late then, won't it?"

"I'm afraid so." Mr. Wilson sighed. "It looks that way."

"No!" I yelled. "We can't give up!"

Mr. Wilson squeezed the steering wheel. "Josh,

there's nothing we can do. We don't know where to look—"

"Just a little farther, please?"

Mr. Wilson looked up the slope. The trail took an even sharper turn up the bank. Only mountain goats risked going further up the slope at this point. "Josh . . ."

"Please?"

"Well," Mr. Wilson grunted. "A little farther, then we turn back and head to camp. Agreed?"

I nodded.

Mr. Wilson leaned forward and gently put his foot on the gas. The Jeep lurched forward a little. It was clearly tough going here. The Jeep had to pick its way at every spot.

I glanced back up at the condors. The sight of them made me sick to my stomach.

Mr. Wilson angled the Jeep past one boulder, and then the right front wheel started to tilt over a second. The Jeep was just starting to ride down on the boulder when it gave way, causing the Jeep to lurch backward violently.

The rear of the Jeep slid over the side of an embankment. In a blur, I saw Mr. Wilson frantically gunning the engine to try to get the Jeep back on level ground. But just as quickly he lost the fight, and the Jeep lurched even further over the embankment.

And then it turned. As the rear tires slid off down the bank, the whole Jeep just rolled. It happened so fast.

"Hold on!" Mr. Wilson yelled.

I grabbed the armrest and ducked my head inside

the Jeep. It lurched to the left, and the side of the Jeep slammed once, hard, into the embankment and rolled over. I had my eyes closed tight, and I could feel myself starting to black out.

The Jeep did a complete flip. Its nose smashed into the turf and kept rolling. It flipped one more time. There was a violent shudder as it careened into a tree and came to a stop, with Mr. Wilson's side facing the ground.

I climbed out over the top quickly, unhurt. I'd banged my head a couple of times during the roll, and my arm had a couple of scrapes, but that was it. The seat belts had held us securely. I hurried around to Mr. Wilson's side.

His car door had been flung open during the roll, and I could see right off that he'd been thrown partially out of the Jeep during the roll. One of his arms was pinned under the Jeep, through the open door. His breathing was shallow when I got to his side.

Mr. Wilson's eyelids fluttered open. There was terrible pain on his face. "It's broken," he whispered. "My arm is caught. I . . . I can feel it. Broken." His eyes closed.

"Mr. Wilson," I said frantically. "What can I do? Please, tell me, what can I do?"

He didn't answer for a long time. He just lay there, his face a pale mask and his breathing so shallow I couldn't tell if he was still alive or not. But he finally answered me. "Try to move the Jeep."

I walked over to the side. I put my shoulder into it and pushed with all my might. It didn't budge, even an inch. The Jeep was wedged up tight against a big pine on one side, and I couldn't push it uphill in the opposite direction. There was just no way.

"Mr. Wilson, I can't," I finally said, winded. "I just can't. I'm sorry. It won't move at all."

"Try the radio," he said, his voice a small whisper.

I looked in the Jeep. The radio had been yanked free of the metal clip that held it in place while the Jeep was moving. I picked it up. The casing had been crushed, probably during the roll. I pushed the switch and got dead air. It didn't work.

"The radio's broken," I said. "What do I do now?"

Mr. Wilson groaned. It was clear he was in a huge amount of pain. I didn't have time right now to feel horrible about the fact that I'd urged him to come up this way.

He opened his eyes again. I looked at him and waited. "Josh, there's a gun . . . in my holster . . . between the seats," he said slowly, each word painful. "Take it. Go back to camp. Get help. You have an hour of sunlight left. It's five or six miles to camp. You can make it. Bring help."

Then he closed his eyes and he didn't open them again. I was beginning to panic.

But I obeyed silently. I knew Mr. Wilson was right. I couldn't move the Jeep myself. There was no way they'd come looking for us up here before dark, and Mr. Wilson couldn't just stay here underneath that Jeep through the night. I had to go get help.

God, I prayed silently, *we haven't talked much. I don't usually ask you about things. I haven't really wanted to. But please help me. Help Mr. Wilson.*

I'm so very, very sorry I made him come up here. I just wanted to help that little boy.

And then I made a deal with God. At least, that's the way I saw it. I know, I know. People do that sort of thing all the time. But I meant it. I did.

The deal was this: if God helped me through this, then I'd pay more attention. I'd ask more questions, listen to Mom more, see what was what, read a little of the Gospels about Jesus' life. That was the deal. I knew it was lame, but it was all I had to offer.

I knew what Mom said, of course. That all God wanted you to offer Him was *yourself.* There wasn't anything else He wanted—not your money, or your good deeds. Just you.

"Give Jesus your life, and you'll get it back," Mom had said once. "That's what you have to pay attention to."

OK, Mom, I vowed, *that's what I'll pay attention to if God helps me out of this jam. I promise. I'll pay attention.*

I clambered over the seat and looked for the holster. It was jammed between the two seats like Mr. Wilson had said. I pulled the holster free and climbed to the ground. I unhooked the leather strap that kept the gun in place and slid it out. It was heavy.

I tried to pull the trigger back. It wouldn't move. "I . . . I, um, can't move the trigger," I mumbled.

"Look on the side," Mr. Wilson whispered. "There's a catch. You have to release it. It's called a safety."

I looked on the side. There was some sort of a catch. I moved it forward, and then tried the trigger.

This time it clicked back into place, ready to fire. I pulled it back a second time and eased it back to where it had been. I put the safety catch back in place and put the gun back in the holster. Quickly, I put the holster around my waist. I had to double it up to make it fit me.

"I'll be back as soon as I can," I said. Mr. Wilson barely acknowledged me with a feeble wave of his free hand. I left in a hurry. I couldn't even imagine what it felt like to have a Jeep crushing your arm. And I didn't want to think about it anymore.

The sun had already dipped below the mountains, so it was starting to get dark even as I set off. I began to jog down the path, avoiding the boulders.

But within minutes, it seemed, it grew harder and harder to follow the path. As dusk began to settle in, I found that I had to look closely to keep to a path that really didn't even seem to be there anymore.

I kept going downhill. But with each step, I began to grow more worried. And then I started to get panicked. I wasn't sure anymore if I was even on the path. Everything was starting to look the same. I *thought* I was moving down through openings between the trees. But I couldn't be sure.

There was tall grass and weeds and boulders everywhere. It seemed like there was a path. But I just couldn't be sure. So I kept going. I had no choice, really.

I started to figure in my mind what could happen if I was off the path and just wandering down the side of a mountain. The worst thing, I figured, was that I'd get to the bottom without any clue where I was. But I could just turn to the left and get to the camp, somehow, couldn't I? And if I fired the gun in the air a few times, maybe they'd come find me?

I started to run faster. Then I almost broke out into a sprint, every hair on the back of my neck starting to bristle. I was lost. No question about it. There was no more path. I'd wandered away from it a long time ago.

The trees started to blur on my left and right. I tripped and stumbled over tree roots and fallen branches. Once, I pitched headfirst, but I scrambled back to my feet quickly and kept running. I *had* to keep going, no matter what. Mr. Wilson was counting on me. I just had to get to the camp.

As the gloom of dusk deepened even further, unseen tree branches whipped my face, raising welts. I was certain I was bleeding in some places by now, but I didn't care. Nothing mattered, except getting to the bottom of this mountain as rapidly as I could.

I started running at nearly full speed. I was moving blindly, hoping against all hope that the slope would start to flatten out soon and that I would be somewhere I could recognize and turn toward the camp. I tried to push the cascading doubts and fears from my mind and concentrated on making sure I didn't smash headfirst into a tree.

I was running so fast, and paying such close attention to the trees directly in front of me with each step, that I wasn't looking around me through the trees. Somewhere, in the back of my mind, I probably took some notice of the gray masses that were evident through the trees on both sides, but I wasn't paying attention.

I came to a creek as the slope started to flatten

out. Finally! I was nearing the bottom. Hope started to flood through me. I jumped the creek joyously and ran even faster. The trees thinned out a little, and then I came to a clearing—

And stopped dead in my tracks. Towering before me were three cliffs. I'd run down into a box canyon. I fought back the tears. "No! No! No!" I cried out.

The box canyon had a strange shape to it. The top of the cliff wall facing me directly had a large bulge near the top. The walls to either side were quite rounded, both at the top and the bottom. They jutted out and then curved in, forming semicircles as they came to the ground. *Probably where rivers had once run,* I figured. It was an odd-looking formation. Even as I tried to push the panic away, I couldn't help but notice how strange it was.

The formation vaguely reminded me of something. There was something, some conversation or picture . . . But I couldn't place it. What was it? I glanced at the formation again. It looked like something, some creature. One of those mountain sheep with the big horns, maybe? Yeah, that was it. Like the head of a bighorn sheep, from the back.

I stumbled over to the closest cliff and looked off in both directions. The cliff walls receded in both directions. I couldn't see the end of them in either direction. They probably went off into the distance for a mile or so, I figured.

I knew I now had two choices. I could either work my way up the slope and try to come back down the mountain once I'd cleared the canyon walls, or I could try to scale the middle cliff wall right here.

I looked up the cliff wall in the center. There were

clearly handholds. I stepped back from it a little, blinking furiously to keep the tears away. The cliff wall wasn't so high. I could do it. I knew I could.

And I sure didn't want to turn around and go back *up* the mountain. So I'd climb the wall, and hope for the best.

I reached up and grabbed an outcropping of rock. I pulled myself up and looked for a place to put my foot. Fortunately, the cliff wasn't a straight vertical. Because I hadn't gotten to the bottom of the mountain just yet, the cliff was actually on a very slight slope, which made the climbing easier.

I moved from outcropping to crevice to outcropping. Actually, there were lots of them—crevices and small shards of rock all over the cliff face. It was more a matter of choosing which place to hold onto and where to step than anything else.

I didn't have time to test each step or handhold. I just had to hope that one of the rocks I chose didn't come loose. One more prayer went winging heavenward.

As I got higher on the cliff, I decided to quit looking down. That made the job harder. I only paid attention to the next handhold, or the next step.

The rustling was off in the distance at first. Then it grew louder, and more insistent. And it began to get closer.

When it was quite close, I finally risked a look around to see what was happening. I nearly fell when I did.

There were condors everywhere. They were circling lazily just a hundred feet or so above me. And there were now dozens of them, circling back and forth and around each other in the sky. They were so close I could see their ugly bodies quite clearly.

An uncontrollable shudder swept through me. Why were they here? What was happening?

The condors were unbelievably larger up close. Their wingspan was twice as long as me, I guessed. They had long, skinny necks. Their ugly heads were covered with tufts of feathers that stuck out in all directions. Their purple plumage was lumpy.

I turned back to my task. I didn't have time to wonder too much about why they were here. I'd deal with that when I got to the top.

The rustling got louder, closer, more insistent. I could hear the flapping of the condors' wings now. They were starting to circle nearer to the cliff. Nearer to me.

And then I felt something on my shoulder. A hard beak. It just nipped at my shoulder. I turned in horror and watched as a condor drifted away from the cliff. It had tried to bite me, or poke at me!

More condors, emboldened by the success of the first, began to circle toward me. Frantically, I looked for a solid place to hold onto with one hand so I could swipe at the condors as they came in toward me. What in the world was going on here?

Several more of the ghastly birds came at me. They were starting to swarm now. I caught one in the neck as it got close. I almost lost my perch, but the bird flew off. I managed to hit a second in the body, forcing it to veer off.

That was enough, for the time being. None of the other birds risked getting too close, so I began to climb again. But I knew I didn't have much time. I had to get to the top fast.

I looked up. My heart leaped. I could see space, maybe twenty feet or so above my head. I was getting there! I reached out for another handhold and pulled myself up. Four or five more and I'd be there.

The condors came back en masse just as I neared the top of the cliff wall. They came in twos and threes. They were clearly determined to keep me from reaching the top of the cliff, for some reason.

I hugged the cliff with all my might. I didn't know what else to do. If I tried to keep climbing, they'd almost certainly knock me off. Their beaks were powerful. They pulled at my shirt when they had the chance.

More and more birds were starting to circle in. Soon, I'd have no choice. I'd have to risk climbing the last couple of handholds in the midst of this sea of condors. I knew I didn't stand a chance of making it before one or more of the birds knocked me loose, but I had to try.

I steeled myself for one final push. My hands trembled. I took a deep breath, looked up one last time, and mapped out my route. Two more rock shards, I figured, and I could pull myself over the top.

The loud *"Screeee!"* came from way off. But the second one was much closer. I jerked my head around. The condors fluttered and wobbled. Something had scared them. What was it? What could possibly spook these foul creatures?

And then I spotted it, racing down toward me like a bolt of lightning. It was a huge bird, easily as large as one of the condors. Its wings were pinned against its sides as it plummeted to the earth.

It pulled up hard as it neared the cliff. The bird spread its magnificent wings and circled them backward, and then practically dove into the cliff, in my direction. It was an eagle. Huge, majestic, bigger than life.

The condors scattered, the rustling of their wings noisy. The eagle flapped its large wings several times to rise up into the sky again and then dove a second time. More condors scattered.

I didn't hesitate this time. The eagle's charge had given me the opening I needed. I reached out and pulled myself the final few feet to the top of the cliff. I clambered over the edge and crawled about five feet or so away from the edge. I collapsed and lay there, my breath coming in ragged heaves.

The condors were still there, but they were more wary. They weren't as close now. I lifted my head enough to see the eagle glide gracefully off to one side and settle onto a limb at the top of a nearby evergreen. The eagle, too, was waiting for something.

When I heard the low, menacing growl close by, I knew what they were all waiting for. In a flash of recognition, the words of the old Indian woman came back to me. The ram's head! That was what the cliff formation reminded me of. That was what I couldn't quite place.

I lifted my head and looked. I had, indeed, stumbled onto the place of the bear.

△

CHAPTER 19

△In one startling mo-
ment, it all made sense to me. Everything. All at
once. Why the condors were circling. Why the eagle,
even, had arrived. They were waiting for the kill. It
was a ritual as old as the Earth itself. And I had
wandered into the middle of it.

I knew, from some distant lesson or TV show,
that all manner of creatures would descend on a
place when a kill was about to be made. Lions, hye-
nas, and vultures would all fight over scraps on the
plains of Africa. It was no different here.

Not more than fifteen feet from me, a huge, hulk-
ing black bear was hunkered over an inert form on
the ground. Here at the top of the cliff wall, there
was more light. I could see the valuable prize the
bear was guarding.

It was the little boy. I was absolutely certain of it.

The boy wasn't moving. I couldn't see if he was breathing or not.

I fought back the tears. Every nerve in my body screamed with pain and anger and fright. This wasn't right. It just wasn't.

Oh, God, where are you? I cried out in silent anguish.

The bear lowered its nose to the ground and let out a low, menacing growl. It looked like it was about to charge. If it did, there was nowhere for me to go. I was every bit as cornered as the bear was.

Then I remembered the gun. It was still strapped to me. I'd forgotten about it. As slowly as I could manage, I reached down and unhooked it. The *snap* as it came undone sounded like a cannon shot.

I pulled the gun free and felt for the safety catch on the side. I eased it forward, and then brought the gun in front of me in slow motion. The bear started to rise on its haunches. I was certain it would charge me at any moment.

But before I could do anything with the gun and before the bear could come at me, there was a loud crashing sound from off to the side. The leaves and branches shook. There was another mighty crash.

The largest creature I'd ever seen came rushing out of the forest, into the clearing at the top of the ram's head cliff. It came at us on two legs. It had to be ten feet tall, maybe more. It let out a mighty roar, shaking the treetops. I screamed.

It was another bear, easily twice as large as the first that was hunkered over the little boy. The second bear charging at us was light gray on top. Its coarse gray hair had white tips. It had a massive, squarish head with a reddish mane. Its legs were dark, dark gray.

It was a grizzly. The old woman had been right. There *was* one last grizzly left in these parts of the Sierra Nevadas.

The grizzly stopped when it had crashed free of the branches. It remained there on both hind legs towering over us. It let loose with another roar.

The black bear couldn't decide what to do now. Should it rush me, or its new challenger? Clearly, like the eagle, the grizzly was here to claim the prize, the little boy.

All of the events of the last twelve hours went rushing through my mind. The way I had it figured, the grizzly was the bear on the rampage. It had surely been the grizzly that had raided those camps, mauled the man, and then dragged the little boy up here to the top of the ram's head cliff, its home.

It *had* to be the grizzly. This was the grizzly's home, and the little boy was here. It all made sense. The grizzly must have dragged the boy up here to its home, gone off into the woods for a drink or something, and the other, smaller black bear had come along while it was away. That had to be what happened.

I raised the gun. I aimed it at the grizzly towering so close. I had no idea whether the gun would do anything, but I had to at least try something before the grizzly chased the black bear off and then mauled me. I cocked the trigger.

But before I could fire it, I remembered. What had the old woman said? That grizzlies can't climb trees? Was that it? And the bear that had attacked the man? It had *climbed down* from a tree before it attacked! I'd seen the claw marks on the bark myself.

It wasn't the grizzly. It had to be the smaller black bear. I stole a glance at the black bear, which was starting to shake with its own rage. I noticed for the first time that there were gobs and gobs of spittle flecked everywhere on its chest. It was literally foaming at the mouth.

The black bear glanced back and forth between its two enemies. There wasn't much choice. Even I could see that. I was the much easier foe. No question about it.

The black bear charged. In one lunging leap, it came at me. I held the gun out in front of me and squeezed the trigger as hard as I could, straight at the charging bear. The gun fired, and the recoil nearly sent me backward over the cliff. I caught myself with one hand.

The bullet buried into the black bear's matted chest. The bear stumbled, bellowed with a terrible rage, and then fell onto me. I pushed and heaved with all my might to get out from under it. I rolled free. A claw raked my face.

The black bear jerked to one side, clawing desperately at its chest to get at the bullet. It rocked back and forth, continuing to bellow as it dug at its own chest.

I saw my opening. Without thinking for my own safety anymore, I scrambled straight at the black bear and gave one big shove. The bear rolled once, still clawing at its chest, and then disappeared over the side of the cliff wall with a hideous scream. It crashed to the ground an instant later and bellowed no more.

I had no time to think about what had just happened, though. I turned to face the grizzly. It rose to its full height. I looked up at it. The creature was ten times my size. It could crush me, if it wanted.

Again, the old Indian woman's words came back to me. "The Great Bear knows fear and courage, weakness and strength," she'd said. If you showed weakness or fear, it would devour you.

I looked again at the grizzly with new eyes. I tried not to be afraid. I knew that was impossible, but I had to try.

I got to my feet, my eyes never leaving the grizzly's. I gripped the gun as hard as I could. I raised it slightly. But I could not fire it. I just couldn't.

We looked at each other, the grizzly and I, for as long as nature allows. In the end, it was the grizzly that turned aside. It shook its terrible, massive head once, fell to its front paws, and then galloped off into the forest. It was gone an instant later.

My eyes had embraced the grizzly, as the old woman had said. I was the mightier creature of God, she'd said. And, I guess, I had shown that. I had shown courage and strength, not fear or weakness. The grizzly had recognized it.

But I knew the courage was not my own. It had come from somewhere else, not necessarily within me. Someday, not now, I would have to try to understand it.

I hurried over to the little boy. So many horrors had happened to me. I feared the worst was yet to come.

But, incredibly, the little boy was breathing. His breath came in raspy, jagged fits, but he was alive. There were deep, ugly red gashes and claw marks covering his entire body. Nearly half his body was caked in blood. But he was clearly alive. Unconscious, mercifully, but alive.

The boy, perhaps four or five years old, lay in a crumpled heap on the ground like a rag doll someone had carelessly tossed to one side. One of his arms lay at an odd angle, surely broken. And perhaps a leg as well.

But he was alive. It was all that mattered. I let out a glorious, tearful shout for joy. I raised my hands in exultation, with only the eagle and the remaining vultures as my witness.

I brought the gun out again and fired three shots into the air. I shouted more, just in case anyone was nearby. Within seconds, my shouts were answered.

The rangers had heard me. I was close enough to the camp that they had recognized my shouts. They would be here soon. It would be all right.

"You're gonna be fine," I whispered to the little boy. I didn't care whether he heard me or not. It felt wonderful just to be able to say the words out loud. "You'll be home soon. I promise."

About the Author

Jeff Nesbit is the author of many books for children and teenagers, including *A War of Words*, *The Sioux Society*, and *The Great Nothing Strikes Back*. He lives with his wife and their three children in Virginia.